TERROR NEAR TOWN

A Harbison Mystery

James R. Wilder

Terror Near Town

terrorneartown.com

jamesrwilder.comjames.r.wilder@att.net

facebook.com/jamesrwilder

james.r.wilder@att.net

ISBN-13: 978-1977747679

ISBN-10: 1977747671

Second Edition

Acknowledgements

My love of the legendary cowboy probably began as I watched the Lone Ranger on and old Admiral black and white console TV at home, and all the TV Westerns and movies that followed. As a news writer and editor I'd been asked numerous times if I had plans for writing "the great American novel." My answer was always "No." The reasoning was simple. Although I have always had a love for westerns, many on TV were filled with flaws of inaccuracies either from lack of information or budgetary restraints. The one I noticed most often was the rectangular hay bale popping up in the 1870s Old West when in actuality the modern-day baler wasn't available until the 1930s. Western novels were much more in tune with the times with Owen Wister setting the standard for many authors when he wrote The Virginian, A Horseman of the Plains. But those novels took place in Texas, Arizona and Wyoming— places where I had limited knowledge of the terrain and customs. After years of rejecting the idea for a western novel a quote from President Theodore Roosevelt came to mind: "Do what you can, with what you have, where you are." The result is Terror Near Town.

There was one place I did know about, a small Missouri town southwest of St. Louis. I had spent much of my teenage years there and had soaked in much of the areas history and folklore thanks to the two who I dedicate this book to: Mrs. Helen Weber and Mr. Jack Lee.

Special thanks for encouraging me on this effort go to my longtime friend Steven W. Weber and my editors G. A. Johnson, Darrin Hull and Barney Denton. Vickie Wheeler gets a tip of my Stetson hat for designing the cover and formatting the book. Many others, including my family, who gave me time to write, are on the top of the list for acknowledgments. Special thanks also go out to: Randy Cate, Glenn Cole, Mike Cole, Jack Elliot, Clem Gruen, Joe Keck, Thomas Langer, Dan R. Manning, Jake Wieberg, the late Ed Wilder, and Michael Wilder.

BACK IN MISSOURI

A locomotive lumbered into Union Station pulling a long line of passenger cars dripping dew from their sides. Chet Harbison looked out the window as the conductor shouted, "All out for St. Louis." Black smoke hovered over the length of the train as it crept under a covered pavilion making it feel like a cave. As he stuck his head out the window to see more, he was hit with the smell of burning coal and the steam oozing from the side of the engine in front of him. To Chet, it seemed like the train was taking its last breath, like that of a man who had run so far that he could run no more and was about to collapse. Chet knew that feeling.

His ride from New York to St. Louis had been filled with transfers and delays that included rail repairs and being switched to sidetracks so "important" express trains could make their schedule. But his journey was finally coming to an end. For the past hour he had been reading a day-old copy of The Chicago Daily Tribune that someone had left behind on the uncomfortable, barely padded, wooden seat. The September 21, 1898 headlines were unimpressive, at least to Chet. A congressman complained that the U.S. intervention in Cuba was unnecessary since Spain was about to lose control of the island anyway because of the lack of funding and had "whipped itself." Other politicians criticized the army for not protecting its soldiers from disease. Chet scoffed at both topics, but the second reminded him to chew on a piece of tree bark he had stashed in a pouch in his pocket. The comment was preposterous in his mind. Colonel Roosevelt did all he could for his troops in the jungles of Cuba; and the Colonel had faced everything all the other soldiers had faced.

The train stopped with a jolt and the passengers stood up and grabbed their satchels from the overhead racks.

Chet rose from his seat and raised his arms above his head and then inhaled a big breath of air. He rubbed the stubble on his chin and brushed back his sandy blond hair and reached for his gear.

He felt relieved that at least the train ride was over. But a different journey was about to begin. He was still forty-five miles from home.

Chet walked outside to the landing and placed his belongings onto the wooden planks and then stretched one more time. His nearly six-foot wiry frame hadn't fit well in the train seats during the cramped journey. By now, the crowd had increased and his fellow passengers shoved him aside as they rushed to get on their way. He bent down and grabbed his belongings—a small, bulged-out duffle bag, a canteen full of water and a rifle stashed inside a saddle scabbard.

Compared to the rest of the crowd, he didn't look well. The Missouri-reared farm boy was easily twenty-five pounds underweight, and despite the cool-morning temperature of about fifty degrees, he was in a constant sweat. His skin and eyes were jaundiced.

I'll feel a lot better once I get home, he thought. He needed fresh air, some home-cooked meals from Lize and Ma, and a feather-bed mattress inside the clapboard farmhouse where he had been born.

For the past nine months his home had been a cot inside a moldy canvas tent in the mosquito-infested jungles of Cuba. Chet was officially a "hero" in the eyes of anyone who had ever read the ongoing stories exploiting Spaniard terrorism— William Randolph Hearst had made sure of that after the sinking of the U.S.S. Maine. Once the news had hit the New York Morning Journal nearly every newspaper in the country had picked up on it. *Hearst got everyone riled up and then the Colonel had to take care of it*, he thought to himself.

Chet was one of Theodore Roosevelt's Rough Riders. The term "Rough Riders" was ironic among the soldiers because most of the horses were left behind in Tampa, Florida, due to lack of space on the steamship. The only "Riders" on horses were officers, and the mules that sailed to Cuba were used as pack animals. The real Rough Riders found themselves in the infantry.

Many a soldier suffered from malaria or yellow (Cuban) fever during their stay on the island, and some of them came home in wooden boxes. The only treatment nurses prescribed for Chet's malaria was bits of tree bark that contained quinine. The effects were minimal when he chewed on a chunk from time to time. *It would just take time*, he thought.

The sprawling city of St. Louis, along the Mississippi, was not new to Chet. He and his father, Byron "Pops" Harbison, along with Chet's older brother, Cody, made regular trips there, selling horses and mules to local dairies, taxi companies, freight haulers and even the police department. The Harbisons had a reputation for providing some of the best stock in the state. Morgan horses and Morgan mules were their specialties. Although every man who had ever dealt with horses had his favorite, nobody denied that the sturdy Morgan was a horse that could get the job done pound for pound. They were stocky for their compact size and could be used for harness or saddle.

Chet took a gander down the street after leaving the train station, trying to familiarize himself with the surroundings. The hustle and bustle of the city wasn't anything like New York where he celebrated the end of the war with members from his outfit but it was a lot busier than the town of Grubville where he'd been born. Peddlers clogged the streets selling everything from fresh fruit, to pots and pans, to rags. There was also a stench in the air from the sun bearing down on the crushed and scattered manure droppings on the street. He knew a street sweeper came through on a regular basis. He was an old man who pushed a large barrel with two wheels attached to the base with a handle on one side of the top of the open container. Attached to the large metal drum were a push broom and a large scoop shovel, much like the one Chet used to clean out the barn stables at his family farm. Unfortunately much of the fresh animal waste clung to the crevices of the cobblestones that were being swept. The smell was constant in almost all the business areas of the city. To him it was a totally different smell than what he was accustomed to at the farm—maybe because it was mixed with the rotted fruits and vegetables that had fallen from vendor carts. The open butcher shops that hung pork and beef sides, and even bear meat, in the open air only added to the aroma. Flies hovered over, but the butchers and the buyers were used to the constant buzzing, and the smell that could cause nausea for some folks.

Chet had cleaned his share of horse stalls over the years but the strong smells in the barns didn't compare to what he smelled on hot city streets. Even if a stall hadn't been cleaned for a week, he could easily walk outside for a fresh breath of air to get away from the strong ammonia smell caused by the mixture of manure and rotted straw.

Chet's flannel shirt was discolored and smelled from the coal soot that sifted through the passenger coach throughout the trip and his face felt like it was coated with the same black film. He walked two blocks east where he spied the old Bowman Dairy. Pops had been selling stock—mainly mules—to the company for some time. Across the street was Glen's Barber Shop. A hot bath, a clean shirt, haircut and a shave would make for a much better morning. He'd find a diner afterward where he could down a decent cup of coffee, some ham and eggs, and maybe even smoke just one of those fancy cigars he had returned with to give Pops and Cody.

Glen was glad to see "the younger Harbison boy". The barbershop was a traditional stop for the Harbison men after they had delivered a string of horses or mules to the city. Glen was raised in the country himself and always enjoyed the stories the Harbisons told about life on the farm. He noted that Cody had been in town about mid-summer, delivering some mules across the street. The barber, who was nearly 80 years old, knew well enough not to make a point about Chet's physical condition and health. He'd been a soldier himself and he'd seen lots of boys comeback from war in worse shape.

"I hope to be home by late tonight if I can grab a ride with one of the freight wagons heading west," Chet said. "I never thought I'd be so happy to get back to that farm where the only noise comes from Ma and old black Lize when we track mud into the kitchen."

And while home may have been a quiet place, downtown St. Louis was getting noisier than what was usual for the bustling city. Just as Glen removed the chair apron and dusted off the hair clippings from Chet's neck, the two heard screaming from a single voice and laughter from many others. Glen and Chet headed for the screen door to see what the racket was about.

Alongside a hitching rail Chet saw a plaid-suited man atop one of the tallest saddle horses he had ever seen. The sorrel's ears were laid straight back as its hooves skidded nervously diagonally across the cobblestone street. A crowd was gathering with workers from the dairy and neighboring businesses. Most were trying to keep from laughing, without success, at the derby-hatted rider. His face was red. He had no control over the horse under him. The more he yanked to tighten the reins the more the horse fought back. Finally when the man loosened his grip for a brief second, the horse reared and flung his head back, hitting the rider square in the face.

Blood ran down from the man's broken nose, but the fat slob wasn't ready to admit defeat. With his left hand grasping the reins, he reached inside to his coat pocket with his right hand and retrieved a pint bottle of bourbon and smashed it between the horse's ears, breaking the bottle. Someone—some fool— had told him that a horse will think the warm whisky to be his own blood and would never toss his head again.

"I'll fix you to mess with me you red-devil son of a bitch!"

The sorrel gelding with two rear white socks likely was thinking the same thing. Owner after owner had attempted to "teach" the horse a lesson with every God-awful trick in the book. The steed would take no more. He reared as high as he could without falling over backwards, all while pawing his front hooves toward the morning sun. The whisky drummer who had been his master for only a few weeks had met his match. He lost his grip and fell onto the paved street. His buttocks and back hit the cobblestones with a thud, and his derby flipped off of his head on impact.

The crowd laughed and jeered. Nearly everyone thought the city slicker from Chicago, who had been pestering saloons for the past several days, had gotten his just dessert.

But the peddler wasn't through. He jumped back to his feet, his disheveled red curly hair now halfway covering his face, and grabbed the reins that dangled from the horse's bridle. With his fist gripping the reins about three feet from their ends, he whipped the horse about the neck and face. The expressions on the faces in the crowd went from smiles to frowns of horror.

Chet had seen enough and rushed down the steps to the street.

"That's no way to treat good horseflesh!"

His snarl cleared a path through the crowd. He grabbed the city slicker by the collar and threw him back down to the cobblestone street. This time the drummer fell flat on his ass. With a surprised look on his face, the horse torturer turned his vengeance toward Chet.

"I paid sixty dollars for that bastard horse and I can do any damn thing I please, you hunk-of-horse-shit hayseed!"

Chet held his fist ready to coldcock the despicable excuse of a human being, but instead, he caught himself short of throwing a punch. He peeled several bills out of his wallet and threw them to the pavement.

"Here's seventy bucks to cover the horse and the saddle! Find a trolley car to sit your fat ass in and stay away from horses!"

The man was tempted to continue the fray, but saw a beat cop smiling with the rest of the crowd.

"It's the best sale I've ever made and the worst buy you'll ever make," the battered dandy howled as he picked up his dented derby and placed it back on his head. He hurried down the street holding the palm of his right hand over the center of his lower back.

Glen started to clap his hands. "Let's hear it for this young Rough Rider from Missouri for setting that city slicker straight," he shouted.

Everyone on the sidewalk followed Glen's lead and applauded.

Chet reached again into his wallet to pay for his bath and haircut.

"The rest of your money is no good here today," Glen said as he placed both palms of his hands in front of the soldier's face as if to push him away. Your little stunt was a lot better than any minstrel show I've ever paid good money for."

Chet blushed as the crowd continued to clap, tipped his Volunteer Army slouch hat to them, and then took ginger steps to keep from spooking the tall gelding. The horse's ears were still straight back and his entire body was quivering. Blood flowed from each side of the horse's mouth and also seeped from the top of his head, and from the lashes on his neck.

"Easy son," Chet whispered as he slowly picked up the reins, being extra careful not to make any sudden movements.

"You're no red devil. You're a fine steed."

Next to the dairy Chet spied the tobacco shop where Pops bought the "makin's" for his corncob pipe. Out on the sidewalk stood a wooden Indian painted in bright colors.

"You're no red devil," Chet quietly repeated. "You're a proud chief—you're Chief Red Man."

The horse's ears briefly flipped forward as if to say thanks. With that, Chet led the long and lanky horse down the alley to the stable entrance of the dairy. He knew Tom Langer, the dairy's stable master, would be obliged to lend him a stall to check out the battered animal. Inside the barn, he found his family friend, who was holding a shovel in his hand while looking at the mess a stable hand had left after he had told his boss that all the stalls had been cleaned. When he looked up at Chet his frown turned to a friendly grin.

"Well, I'll be darn. If it ain't Chet Harbison, back from Cuba," he said.

"Hi Mr. Langer. I need to ride this horse back home, but he's going to need some tending to. Can you help?"

Langer reached out his large hand to shake.

"You know that I will do anything I can to help a Harbison," he said. "I take it that this long-legged critter had something to do with all that shouting going on outside?" he said, as he looked the horse over. "From what I heard from here, I hope you don't talk that way in front of your mother. Golly, your pa is going to have a conniption fit when he sees you ride in on this tall drink of water. He must be sixteen and a half hands high. Those Morgans are going to look awfully short in comparison."

Chet grinned, but the grin turned to shock as he removed the gelding's bridle. The horse continued to tremble.

The curb chain was so tight that he wasn't even able to slide his pinky finger between it and the horse's chin. Even worse, someone had used a bicycle bit and both corners of the horse's mouth were raw. The bit's name couldn't have been described any better. A six-inch length of safety chain from the latest bicycles, which replaced the high-wheel models, was attached to each arm of the bit.

"I've got some pine-tar salve we can put on that," Tom said. "He may not like the taste, but his mouth will feel much better in the morning. But first, lets get him some water, some fresh oats and hay. This poor animal is close to skin and bone."

"His hooves are past due for trimming and he needs new shoes," Chet said while attempting to lift the rear left hoof. The horse jolted and tried to kick. The former soldier knew he was in for some difficulty.

Langer had been watching how carefully the young man had attempted to deal with the skittish animal.

"I don't want to put a twitch on him," Chet said. "I've never seen a horse's mouth look as torn up as his."

"You're going to have to loop a Scotch hobble on him, boy, or you'll never get him shod."

"I can't put him through that," Chet said. "He's been through hell and back. He doesn't need to be knocked off balance and put down on his side."

"We don't have to go that far, boy," Tom said, "and we don't have to get kicked in the head either."

The tall and burly man grabbed an inch-thick rope hanging on the wall with his calloused hands and made a loop around the gelding's left rear ankle and then tethered the other end of the rope onto the loose halter the horse was now wearing.

"See, I'm tightening the rope just enough so he has to lift that hoof a couple inches off the ground. That gives you the room you need to trim it and put a new shoe on. When you finish the rear hooves, we'll put his saddle back on. We'll put a loop around one of his front ankles and then wrap the other end of the rope around the saddle horn—just enough to lift that hoof. He may feel a little off balance, but he won't be able to kick, and he'll feel a lot better with four new shoes."

The procedure took longer, much longer, than any farrier work Chet had ever performed, but in all honesty, he believed it was the best job he had ever completed. By now Chet's face and shirt were drenched with sweat.

Tom returned to inspect the job. Then he sat down on a wooden crate and opened his lunch pail, removing a thick Braunschweiger sandwich that he quickly tore in half, offering a portion to Chet. Then he reached for a bucket filled with Griesedieck Brothers beer he had kept cool sitting inside a washtub filled with ice chunks from one of the milk wagons.

"I'm surrounded by milk bottles, but milk is for children," Tom said. He took a pull of beer and smiled. "It's way too late for you to leave for Grubville this afternoon. Why don't you stay at my place like you do when you bring us mules? Margie will have something good for us for supper, and this long-legged purchase of yours can get some rest. He'll need it for that long trip home, and I believe you do too."

For the remainder of the afternoon, without being asked, Chet worked in the stable just as he would have done chores back at the farm. Stalls were mucked and harnesses and tack were repaired and cleaned with saddle soap. Chet helped Mr. Langer shoe one of the more cantankerous mules and barely avoided being kicked when he lifted the animal's left rear hoof.

"This cuss deserves a twitch in his mouth for all the spite he's got boiling up inside of him," Chet said with a chuckle.

"He'll settle down in a spell," Mr. Langer said. "The owner of the dairy is bringing his son-in-law 'up through the ranks' so to speak, so he's started him off having him delivering milk before he gets that cushy job up in the office where they go out to lunch everyday and smoke cigars. He's been taking out his grief on this old broom tail for the past several weeks now because he was thinking he should go to the front office his first day on the job. I don't like it when someone starts messing with my mules. This old boy has been pulling a milk wagon for going on ten years and I've never gotten a complaint out of any of the driver's. But I bet I get one out of my future boss today. I had the boys hitch up the rankest mule I could find for him this morning. And that mule is dumber than a middle horse pulling a fire wagon. You might say I 'fixed his wagon!'

"Son, you've done more work around this place in the past day than that stable boy I fired did all week," Tom said. "Check out that gelding of yours one more time and let's head home for supper."

Chet walked down to the far end of the barn and whispered as he entered the stall but Red's ears went straight back when Chet opened the horse's mouth, even though he did it the same way as if he was opening an infant's mouth to check for teething. He spread another thin layer of salve on the open sores.

"You may not think much of me yet, boy, but you will if you just give it a chance. Tomorrow's going to be a challenge for both of us."

HEADING HOME

Chet and Mr. Langer arrived back at the dairy early the next morning before six o'clock. Chet helped him with harnessing the mules to the milk wagons while delivery drivers filled the backs of the wagons with blocks of ice and wire baskets containing six quart bottles of fresh milk. Before starting off, Chet helped Mr. Langer with his morning chores.

Both men watched with some amusement as the owner's son-in-law made a wide circle around the skittish mule hitched to his wagon and then kept his eye on the mule's rump as he climbed into the seat, not wanting to be kicked. He and the ornery mule left the barn for what would be a long day for both of them.

Chet and the stable master both started laughing as soon as the wagon was out of sight.

"Well, enough of that," Langer said. "I imagine I'll be retired by the time that young whipper snapper is put in charge of me.

"You know Chet, you don't have to ride that horse home today, even though I think he can make, " Mr. Langer said. "My mule is broke to saddle as well as harness and you could borrow him for a week or two and just lead that horse of yours with a halter and a rope."

"Yeah, but I don't think that's what I want to do," Chet said. "He needs to get to know me and I need to get to know him. I don't think that would happen with me tuggin' on that rope for pert near forty miles, especially with him lookin' at the east end of a southbound mule, iffen you know what I mean. I'll take it easy with Red and we should be able to make it home by dark. I know this horse has character. I can just feel it in my bones that he's up to the challenge, just like I am.

"Enough said. You're going to need a hackamore bridle for your horse, son. His mouth won't even stand a snaffle bit. Let's see what I've got back in the tack room."

"I'll need a martingale or some other type of tie-down too," Chet said. "Red busted up that drummer's face really good when he threw his head back. I don't need that."

"I can find that too," Tom said as he sauntered to the back of the stable. He returned with a martingale and a hackamore bridle within a moment or two.

"This hackamore is as about as mild as they get," he said. "It's just a nose band with a two-inch wide leather strap with some sheep's wool attached on the side that touches his muzzle. It should be plenty good as long as you don't get him into a run and then have to stop quickly. And I don't think this skin-and-bones horse is up to any type of race right yet, anyway!"

Chief Red Man looked a little more at ease when his new owner entered the stall, but his ears went straight back again when he saw Chet approach him with the new bridle.

16

Chet spoke softly as he walked, "This is going to be a lot easier on you, boy. We've got a long ride ahead of us today and you're going to have to learn to trust me. I'm not going to treat you like that fat-assed drummer did. Us Harbisons believe in gentling a horse, not breaking 'em down."

The horse's ears flipped forward for a second or two and then went straight back as Chet placed the saddle on his back and tightened the cinch. He tied the rifle scabbard on the side of the saddle and secured the ties on the duffle bag around the saddle horn. He swung the canteen strap around his neck. And then, Tom handed the young man a worn saddlebag.

"Here's some sandwiches for you and a couple of apples for you and the horse," Tom said.

"I can't thank you enough Mr. Langer," Chet said.

"Don't mention it, boy," Tom said. "It was my pleasure. It should be pretty easy going for you once you get out of the city, but those horseless carriages are starting to show up on the city streets, making all sorts of racket and belching smoke just like a locomotive. One of 'em drove by ol' Dobbin here when he was tethered just outside the stable. I thought that mule was going to jump right out of his harness—took ten minutes to calm him down."

"I'll keep that in mind," Chet said. "Maybe I won't see any this early in the morning. Besides, they won't last. From what I saw in New York those contraptions are broken down more than they run."

"Time will tell son," Tom said. "Don't press that horse too hard, and say hello to your pa for me, and to that strappin' big brother of yours."

They walked the tall horse out to the street with Chet whispering to the animal as he double-checked the bridle and then the saddle cinch. As he attempted to mount the horse, Red got skittish again swinging its rump against the hitching rail with no room to move elsewhere. Instead of saddling up with the horse pinned against the railing, Chet waited until the horse calmed down and moved away from the post.

"Easy boy, we can do this," he said. Then on the second try, Chet slowly hoisted himself onto the saddle. The horse only shied a little this time, but then lifted its front hooves off the ground to show his disapproval. The tie-down prevented the animal from throwing his head back into Chet's face. The young soldier kept the reins loose and patted the horse's neck to let him know that there was no ill will between them—and then Red settled down as much as one could expect for an animal that had been whipped the day before.

Chet started Red at a slow even pace and talked to the animal with a quiet, soothing voice. The first big hurdle would be crossing the Meramec River about fifteen miles ahead. Red would have to ride the ferry across. Chet hoped the boat wouldn't be crowded. Crossing the Big River, closer to home, wouldn't be nearly as challenging, as long as a particular bunch of "river trash" who lived along the banks didn't give them any trouble.

After the first ten miles Chet realized he and Red made a pretty good team. He felt like he could touch a low-hanging cloud sitting atop the animal. Riding a bareback Belgium draft horse back to the Miller Farm was the only other time he had ridden such a tall horse. But that ride had left him bow-legged for several hours. That wasn't a problem with Red. He was too skinny, even for a saddle horse.

The ferry ride at the Meramec went easier than expected. Chet was the only boarder, and while Red was skittish as the muddy water swirled around the flat-bottom boat, they made it to the other side without any major problems. The gelding lunged for the shore when the ferry stopped, but it wasn't anything Chet couldn't handle. Down the road Chet stopped at a general store in an area known only as Murphy Flats. He pumped some fresh water into the trough for his horse and then, began to check the horse's feet for stones. His moves were slow and cautious. As expected the animal was skittish. Finally, he let the soldier lift each hoof and allowed Chet to use his Barlow knife to remove some small stones and caked mud from the bottom of his feet. When finished, Chet patted the horse on his muzzle and gave him one of the apples from his saddlebag. The apple was gone within a few seconds.

Making sure the reins were secured to the hitching post, Chet made his way up the wooden plank steps and entered the store.

"Hi, you got any canvas coats—the kind with the great big front pockets?" Chet asked, as he walked into the dingy store. Piles of clothing, canned goods and farm supplies were strewn across the shelves without rhyme or reason and the storeowner looked as disheveled as the inside of the store.

"Sure, son, but it still feels like summer out there. What the hell do you need a coat for?"

"Ya never know when the weather will change in Missouri," Chet said. "I just want to be prepared."

The store clerk shrugged his shoulders, thinking this young man's "cornbread wasn't baked through to the center." He rifled through the stacks of coats and found one that might fit the skinny young man as much as that was possible.

Chet gave the man his money and walked outside to see the sun bearing down. After rolling up the coat and tying it behind his saddle, he straddled the gelding and continued his journey west at a trot.

Chet made several stops to give the abused horse a rest while he rolled the makin's and smoked a cigarette. He even walked part of the way before the worn and rotted-from-mold Army boots he wore started to give his feet trouble. Chances were that he wouldn't make it home until after dark. Chief Red Man was a determined horse, but Chet could tell he was fatigued—and so was Chet.

A cool breeze from the west fanned his face in the morning but by noon Chet began to sweat. The fall breeze stirred the dust amongst the falling leaves, and Chet's face and arms. There were only a sampling of farmhouses along the way, but when they appeared Chet made a point to stop and let Red have a drink of water and cool down. Most of the farmers were familiar with the Harbison family, and none turned away a stranger, much less a soldier coming back from war. Many of the older farmers knew of too many whom never returned after leaving the area wearing blue or gray uniforms nearly four decades earlier.

By the time Chet was just shy of the Big River, he eased the ends of the reins up to his chest, pulling the gelding to a stop. He dismounted and loosened the saddle cinch. There was some dry Timothy grass along the dirt road and he let Red take advantage of it. As the horse grazed Chet opened the duffle bag and reached inside to the various pieces of rolled clothing inside the sack and retrieved a Colt .45 Peacemaker. He opened the gate and confirmed that the only empty chamber was under the hammer. He untied the farm coat from behind the seat of the saddle, put it on and slid the revolver inside the right-hand pocket.

After retightening the cinch he was back in the saddle and on his way. As he approached the river he saw just what he expected—one of the Spragg brothers. It was the youngest of the four. The skinny runt of a kid was tall for his age and his oily face was already full of pockmarks and pimples. He looked as if he hadn't bathed in months and the smell coming from his body backed up Chet's thoughts. Even Red's nostrils took notice of the body odor and flared open.

"Well, if it ain't that skinny soldier boy back from the war on a skinny horse ta boot," Lester Spragg said. "You don't look too good, Harbison."

Lester Spragg was only about 13 years old. Raised by his three older brothers, he appeared to be picking up their same smart-ass personalities.

The only thing the youth had been "learned" was how to steal, Chet thought to himself. A good whoopin' in a woodshed and someone taking the boy in would be Lester's only chance for a decent life.

But that was somebody else's problem. Chet wanted to get home. The soldier's hand was already inside his right pocket with the hammer pulled back when he approached the boy.

"You're on old man Potter's land at this crossing and he's chargin' two bits for anyone to cross. I'm in charge of this operation," the boy said with his outstretched hand quivering, "so hand over the money."

"Otis Potter would give anybody four bits just to come and see him now that his wife is dead," Chet said.

He removed the revolver from in his coat pocket and pointed the weapon just below Lester's belt buckle.

"You tell that peckerwood brother of your'n to come out from behind that oak tree, holding that shotgun by the end of the barrel," Chet said. "If he don't, this horse ain't goin' to be the only gelding on this here riverbank."

The look of dominance on Lester's face turned to one of fright. "Alberrrt! Do what he saaays!"

Albert Spragg came out from behind the tree and shrugged as he handed the single-shot shotgun to Chet with the stock pointed at the rider. For some reason, Red remained still, not jittery like he was the day before—maybe it was the confidence in Chet's voice, maybe the horse was just tired. Chet broke open the barrel and removed the single shell, throwing it into the river. Then he tossed the shotgun to the ground.

"Now both of you, empty your pockets and throw any shells you have into the river," he said.

They followed his orders.

"You may think you're one smart son-of-a-bitch, Harbison, but this wouldn't-a ever happened if Luke and Dutch hadda' been here too," Albert said.

Chet said nothing and coaxed Red into the shallow stream. The worst of the day was over. The cool water felt good on Red's hooves, and on Chet's feet. If it wasn't the Spraggs it would have been someone else. It seemed like the river bottoms drew some of the worst "stump jumpers" there were. They were always trying to get something for nothing, and oftentimes did. Chet had had his share of problems with the Spraggs and he knew there would likely be more. It was just a matter of time that someone—someone who had had enough of them—would decide those boys didn't need to breathe anymore. They were the type that reminded him of a kid poking a stick at a dog chained up to a stake—they were always asking for it.

The short drink and the cool water on Red's legs provided the horse just what he needed—a second wind. His pace picked up for the next several miles, but Chet continued to make stops along the way to let Red drink and rest. Chet always tipped his hat to farmers who were harvesting their crops or tending to livestock in the fields. Almost everyone waved and gave a long stare at the long-legged horse and the soldier on his back.

The last leg of the trip seemed more relaxing for Chet. His anxiety diminished after crossing the Big River, but so had his strength. He was tuckered out and by the time he left the main road and had turned south his eyelids began close and then reopen when Red stumbled on the rougher terrain that led to Chet's hometown. After what seemed like an eternity, Chet reached a faded white sign with black letters— Grubville, Population 50. No one was really sure where the name came from. Some said it was the last place to stop for provisions for a long while. Others claimed that the first homesteaders called it Grubville because of all the grub worms they found when they first plowed the meadows for planting.

Regardless, it wasn't much of a town. There was a general store on the east side of the street that also doubled as a post office. Across the street was Wheeler Frost's feed store and tavern. Wheeler was a soft-spoken man of nearly seventy. He also was the one to see if you needed a shotgun, rifle or pistol. Folks believed he made more from that business than the other two combined. Wheeler also was one of the few who had a telephone, but it was treated like public property. Anyone who needed to make a call to the city was allowed to and they would leave a nickel or dime on the bar. Down the road another quarter mile was the schoolhouse that Chet had attended up until the eighth grade. It doubled as a church on Sunday. About once a month a circuit-riding preacher would hold a service. When he wasn't there, one of the farmers would stand behind the pulpit and read from the "good book" for about thirty minutes or so. Some in the congregation believed the reading should last at least an hour.

By now Red's head was drooping almost to the ground. The horse's chest and legs were coated with sweat and dust, as were Chet's pants. He was exhausted as well. His shoulders were slumped forward as the horse prodded up to the tavern's hitching rail.

"Is that you Chet?" Wheeler asked as he squinted into the darkening sky. "Your ma and pa have been wondering when you were going to make it back. But you better come in for a piece."

The old man took the reins and tied them to the railing and then scampered about bringing back a half-full bucket of water to the horse.

"Not too much Mr. Frost, I don't want him to get sick," Chet said. "He's awful hot."

"I'll give him just enough to wet his whistle," Wheeler replied. "You need to come in for a spell. How about a cold Falstaff on me? It's a brand-new beer and it's pretty good. I'll throw in a couple of pickled eggs too."

That sounded good to Chet. It had been hours since he had eaten the sandwiches packed by Mrs. Langer. Chet stretched his arms out and rolled his neck from one side to the other to ease the stiffness in his body.

"What's that on the side of your saddle, Chet? Looks kinda new-fangled."

"It's a Krag-Jorgensen .30-40 carbine," he said. "It's smokeless. Feel free to give it a look-see. You can even come down to the farm and try it out if you like."

Wheeler gave it a hard looking over and was impressed. "Them cartridges look like they drop into that fancy chamber real easy like," he said.

It was past closing time and the bar stools were turned upside down on the bar. Wheeler pulled two of them down and placed them on the rough-cut oak floor. Then he walked to the opposite side of the bar and filled up a mug from the tap.

Wheeler's store looked like many others throughout the country. A dark-stained oak bar with stools ran the width of the building. Sacks of feed were stacked along the walls and a checkerboard sat atop a wooden barrel. An unlit potbelly stove stood in the center of the room and a pool table was off to the side. Deer antlers lined the tops of the walls and the smell of cigarettes and cigar smoke lingered.

"This beer's pretty smooth," Chet said as he wiped some foam from his mustache."

"Yeah, it's made by Lemp Brewery. They introduced it a while after you left town. I've been sellin' a lot of it on Friday and Saturday nights."

Then Wheeler paused for a moment.

"Chet, I better warn you. There's been trouble down your way," Wheeler said. "The Cavanaugh place burned to the ground and killed 'em all dead about two weeks ago—all except for that little red-headed daughter. Carl and Susan

Cavanaugh and that white housemaid of theirs burned to death. The girl came runnin' down to your folks' place screamin' like she had gone mad. Byron and Helen took her in until they can figure out what to do with her. Half the county would have burned down if it hadn't been for a downpour that followed. It was a real toad strangler."

Chet set his beer down on the counter. His jaw dropped as he started to pay more attention to Mr. Frost's words.

"Is she, is Callie okay now?" he asked. "I can see someone wanting to take a fist to old man Cavanaugh, but why would anybody want to kill him or hurt the rest of his family? Mrs. Cavanaugh was always real quiet, but really friendly, and so was that skinny little Callie. She always had a kind word but acted like she just didn't fit in here. Did you ever notice her green eyes? I don't think I ever saw anyone with green eyes before seeing hers."

"She seems to be doing a little better," Wheeler said. "But she doesn't remember much of what happened. I knew soldiers like that when they came out of horrific battles. Some could talk about their fight and others couldn't or wouldn't talk about it."

The Cavanaughs were a strange bunch compared to most folks around Grubville as far as Chet was concerned. Carl Cavanaugh was a perfect gentleman when he greeted women and families at church or the general store, but he was rude and egotistical when dealing with any of the local farmers or others when it came to business. He claimed to have come from Kansas City and wanted to be a cattle rancher. But his idea of working was to take off his tie and suit coat and order farm hands around on his one-hundred-and-seventy-five-acre spread. Everything he owned seemed expensive—the fancy Studebaker buggy, his clothes, the furniture in his house and even the thick eye spectacles he wore. He was about fifty years old. Many thought he was about five-feet, nine-inches tall, but his belly protruded out so much that most couldn't get close enough to him gauge his height. He must have weighed about the same as Chet's brother, Cody, but was easily five inches shorter. Susan Cavanaugh looked nearly forty. She was small framed, much like her daughter, and was highly educated although she never bragged about it. While most farm kids were through with schooling by the seventh or eighth grade, her mother was still teaching Callie. At least it was still going on when Chet left for the war.

Chet recalled when Carl Cavanaugh first moved to the area about three years earlier, he had pushed his way into Mr. Frost's place one Friday night when all the farmers were in enjoying companionship and draft beer.

"I'd like a single malt," he said as Mr. Frost approached him from the other side of the bar.

"Mr. Cavanaugh, this ain't no ice cream parlor. You're going to have to go all the way to Cedar Hill if you want a malted."

Cavanaugh called Frost a "buffoon" and then went on for minutes explaining that "single malt" was an expensive type of scotch.

"Well, I got a single bottle a rye, two bottles a bourbon and a jug a moonshine from back in the hill country—take your pick," Frost quipped.

The red-faced Cavanaugh left the tavern in disgust and only came back when he was ordering feed for his horses or the purebred Aberdeen Angus cattle that he had brought in for his farm.

By the time Chet finished his beer, it was dark, but the moon was just two days shy of being full. Chet thanked the shopkeeper for the nourishment and mounted Red one last time for the night. Another mile down the way he turned back east onto Harbison Road, named after his grandpa. As he rode by the Cavanaugh place Red's nostrils flared up. Anyone passing there could still smell the charred remains of the house. Finally the weary duo made it to the farm gate. Chet dismounted and pulled a lever that allowed the gate to open without much effort—something his father had designed using weights and pulleys. As he walked the horse through the opening he was greeted by Pebbles, the mixed-breed black and white spotted collie that arrived one day at the farm and never left. Ma had taken him in since he was half starved. The dog didn't bother to bark, but he jumped at Chet. Together, the three walked down the dirt road that led to the farmhouse. Chet could smell the dry haystacks along the field and as he walked he listened to the crushing of the large orange and gold sycamore-tree leaves underfoot. You could smell the hay and leaf dust in the air. He had always liked fall weather. Once the hay was stacked it was a time where the workload eased up just a little before winter set in. The air was still down in the valley that Chet called home. All was calm and only the sounds of crickets could be heard.

The kerosene lamps in the farmhouse were already out. Chet had visited with Mr. Frost for more than an hour. He spoke little about the war, but asked Mr. Frost question after question about the fire and what had been going on while he was away. Chet led the horse to the red barn on the far side of the farmhouse. He found an empty stall next to the Holstein milk cow, removed the bridle and saddle and gave Red a good rub down. Pebbles curled up on the straw-covered dirt floor as if to say he would keep an eye on the new horse.

The farmhouse was dark and Chet didn't want to wake anyone. He removed his rotted leather and canvas boots, leaving them on the front porch, never to be worn again. He opened the screen door and walked through the kitchen and across the hall to the sun porch in the back. There was a cot there—better than the one he had in the army. He took off his shirt and pants, and collapsed onto it. There was no sense stumbling around in the dark to find his room upstairs.

A MORNING TO REMEMBER

Chet woke up early Saturday morning just before sunrise after being startled in his sleep, apparently the first one in the house to see the beginning of the day. Still in his "long handles," he crossed the hall and walked into the kitchen. He tossed some kindling into the stove and started to grind some coffee beans.

What happened next might have been funny if he had been in a sportin' house in New York City, but since it happened at home, it was downright embarrassing for him and the family's new houseguest, Callie Cavanaugh. The sun was beginning to rise as Callie entered the kitchen from the hallway, right in front of the sun porch. Her silky red hair was uncombed and the nightgown she wore was made from cotton flour sacks—probably sewn up by Lize or Ma—for the teenage girl. The bright sun came through the screened porch behind her and showed right through the fabric. Chet didn't have to imagine how the 17-year-old girl had filled out since he had last seen her. At the same time, the young lady couldn't help but stare at the unusual-looking bulge protruding from Chet's long johns, just below his waist on that very early morning.

Both turned red with embarrassment. Callie, who had a dusting of freckles on her face, blushed to the point where her freckles blended with the redness now in her cheeks. She turned away and scampered for her makeshift bedroom down the hall that had been Pops' office. At the same time, Chet turned his back to the girl until she left. After the coast was clear, he returned to the sun porch and put on his britches and shirt. *What a way to start the first morning back home*, he thought.

Callie had raced to the bedroom that Byron and Helen Harbison had rearranged so she could be close to their own bedroom if the young girl continued to have nightmares. She closed the door behind her, being careful not to slam it. Callie stood in front of the mirror and started to brush her long red hair. She was embarrassed, confused and even more, she was curious about what she had just seen.

Ten minutes later, she returned, first peeking around the edge of the doorway to make sure Chet was now properly clothed. She was wearing a blue gingham dress.

"Good morning Chet," she said, avoiding direct eye contact with him. "I didn't know you were home."

"I got in late," he said, acting as if it was the first time they had met that morning. "I'm really sorry to hear about your folks."

There was a pause, where neither knew what to say, but Lize took care of that when she entered the kitchen.

"Oh my God, little Chester is finally home!" she screamed. "Mr. Byron, Mizzez Helen, our little boy is here!"

Chester was the given name that Chet detested, but it never bothered him when Lize said it. The tall and slender big-boned former slave had lived on the farm all but seven or eight years of her life. His smile spread across his face as he greeted her. She ran up to him, giving him the biggest hug he had ever encountered. In fact, he winced and felt a sharp but short pain in his side wrapped her arms around his waste. Seconds later he spied his parents, Byron and Helen Harbison entering the kitchen.

"Welcome home son," Pops said. "I was wondering if you were ever going to make it back from the big city."

Helen Harbison was not one to show emotions with her family. She was always a "matter-of-fact type" of woman, but tears ran down her cheeks as she walked up to hug her youngest son. "I thought I might not ever see you again," she said as she hugged him.

"Hey little brother," was the next greeting Chet heard.

Cody Harbison wrapped his arms around his younger brother like a grizzly bear. He was five years older than Chet, almost a half a head taller and weighed nearly a hundred pounds more. In tow was Cody's wife with "Little Cody" in her arms. Beth, one of the Miller girls, was a buxom gal with dark brown hair. Although a little on the large size, many a man in the county had remarked that she was a "mighty handsome" woman. Cody and Beth were married about a month before Chet left. Little Cody, who looked to be about a month old, was screaming his lungs out.

"Looks like feedin' time for this here youngin'," Beth giggled.

She started to pull down one shoulder of her nightgown and headed for the parlor for some privacy.

Byron Harbison whispered into his wife's ear, "If thar's a lactation relation to breast size, Little Cody will never have to worry about starvin' to death."

Helen Harbison, a much slighter woman in comparison, elbowed her husband in the stomach.

"Hush! She might hear you," Helen said while grinning at her husband's comment.

"You look like you've lost a lot of weight," Helen inquired. "Are you alright?"

"I will be now that I'm home, Ma," he said.

By now Lize was rattling pots and pans and stoking the stove again. Sausage links were being pulled out of the lard can for frying and she was ordering Cody to go out back to the hen house to get some fresh eggs.

"I'll get Chester fattened up Mizzez Helen," she said.

Everyone wanted to know about the war, the trip back home, and the experience Chet had relayed about encountering two of the Spragg brothers the day before. Questions continued for what seemed like forever. Pops did more observation than question asking. Then he got up from his chair, lit his pipe and meandered to the window as Cody returned to the house.

"What in tarnation do you have out in the barn?" Cody asked as he returned with nearly a dozen brown eggs in a basket. "I ain't seen nothin' like it before."

With that, Pops grabbed his cane and proceeded to limp out to the red barn with Cody and Chet.

"Looks like the boy brought back one of them giraffes from Cuba," Pops said with a grin. The fifty-five-year old had always been known for his dry sense of humor.

"They don't have giraffes in Cuba, Pops," Chet replied.

Pops tolerated his son's sarcasm as he expected others to tolerate his own.

"Mr. Langer said he thinks Red's part American Saddlebred and part Thoroughbred."

"He didn't sell this skinny critter to you, did he?" his father asked.

"No, I sorta'—rescued him. I don't think he would have lasted another week under the hands of the bastard who had him," Chet said. "I paid seventy bucks for him and the saddle."

"Nice saddle," Pops said. He tugged the fender with yet another grin. "You're just like your ma, always tryin' to help some poor critter down on his luck."

Chet's father walked up to the horse and started talking to him, much in the same quiet manner that Chet had for the past day. He opened the horse's mouth.

"Looks to be about a four-year-old," Pops said. "What'd that fella use for a bit, a rat-tail file?"

"Even worse," Chet said.

He opened the saddlebag given to him by Mr. Langer and retrieved the bicycle bit.

"Jesus, Mary and Joseph!" Cody said. "Why didn't the son of a bitch just use a piece of barbed wire?"

"I named him Chief Red Man, and he's already coming along," Chet said. "It's just going to take a little time to get his weight back up and have him know that not everyone wants to beat the hell out of 'em, or kill him."

"The same goes for you, too," Pops said. "I bet your ma and Lize have just about got breakfast ready for us." Then he turned to his other son, "Cody, let this string bean of a horse know he can trust you too. Give him some more oats and hay and then open the outside stall door so he can enjoy the sunshine out in the paddock. Boy, he sure is a lanky one!"

When they returned, Ma was placing a bowl of scrambled eggs and plate of fresh biscuits on the table while Lize used a spatula to retrieve the bacon and sausage sizzling on the cast-iron skillet. Hot grease was splattering from the frying pans, but Lize didn't seem to worry about it.

Breakfast couldn't have been finer at the Harbison home. Chet and just about everyone else stuffed themselves with sausage, bacon, biscuits, eggs, fried potatoes and cup after cup of coffee. Lize kept dishing more and more food onto Chet's plate and slapping Cody on the hand any time he tried to reach for a second helping.

There was plenty of food but she would eat at a separate table by the window after the others were served, just as she had done most of her life.

Afterward Cody helped Chet grab his gear and take it to the small bedroom upstairs. Chet opened his duffle bag and pulled out his U.S. Army Volunteer uniform, some socks, long johns and a rolled-up navy-blue pinstripe suit that included a vest, a frilly white shirt and a striped tie. There was even a pair of cufflinks and black wingtip shoes.

"Golly, Chet, that suit looks a tad better than what the preacher wears when he comes to town. It looks like something old man Cavanaugh wears, uh, used to wear."

"It's what they call a Brooks Brothers suit," Chet explained. "I made friends with a high falootin' polo player kid from New York after we got to Cuba. We covered each other's backs during some pretty tough times in the jungle. When the war ended, the steamer took us back to Long Island, not too far from where Ritchie lived. We were supposed to be quarantined, but his old man took care of that pretty darn quick. I got to stay in this big mansion his folks had. There were all sorts of parties going on for us and Ritchie got me this suit—even had a tailor fit it for me. The tailor, Mr. Lewie they called him, said he left it where I could fill it in a little better once I got home."

"So'd this Ritchie fella show you the town? I hear there's all sorts of gals that will do just about anything in those big cities."

"Yea, we met all types of girls, rich ones and ones who wanted to be rich by latchin' onta guys like Ritchie—but they weren't the type of gals I'd wanna' bring home to meet Ma," he said.

Cody and Chet grinned at each other as if sharing an inside joke about what kind of girls Ma would like. Cody couldn't keep his eyes off the Colt or the rifle inside the scabbard.

"How'd you get these?" Cody asked. "The newspaper up at Mr. Frost's said the soldiers had to turn in all their weapons before they were released from duty."

"I got them for shoeing a horse," Chet said. "On March 30, us volunteers were camped out in the jungle. A regular army man, a quartermaster, shouted for "Missouri,"—that's what they all called me—to come over to his side of the camp. He asked if it was true that I knew how to shoe a horse. When I told him I could, he breathed a little easier and told me to get to work on a little chestnut gelding that was tied up nearby. The quartermaster had sent the farrier back to the nearest town for supplies a day earlier. When he got back, he only had half the grub and was drunker than a skunk. He must have been whorin' and drinkin' the whole time he was gone. I saw him passed out in the dirt laying in his own puke. 'I need this horse shod right away or I might be kicked down to buck private for the rest of my career,' he told me.

"The horse looked like one of those little cow ponies we see that comes up from Texas every once in a while," Chet said. "He was pretty sturdy lookin'; had a star on his face and four white socks. They didn't have a forge so I had to cold shoe him. Just about the time I got done, this Lt. Colonel with real thick spectacles comes up and asks the quartermaster if 'Little Texas' is ready. Both of us jumped to attention and he told us to be 'at ease.' He looked at the horse's feet and said, 'deeelightful,' grabbed the horse by the reins and walked off. Turned out the officer was Theodore Roosevelt, second in command of the volunteers under Colonel Leonard Wood. The next day Roosevelt rode that horse up and down San Juan

Hill encouraging us on to kill all them Spaniards that were shootin' down on us. He finally wore the little horse out and had to do the rest of his commanding on foot. But I know for a fact—that little gelding never lost a shoe through all that runnin' back and forth.

"I bet this rifle did the trick when you and your buddies went up that hill," Cody asked.

"Them Spaniards actually had a rifle that would load faster, and they had the advantage over us bein' on top of the hill. The thing that saved our asses was some army regulars with a Gatling gun—and Colonel Roosevelt. For a city slicker that guy had some sand in his craw. He kept encouraging us to keep goin' all the while bullets were flying all around him. When the war finally ended, Ritchie and I were boarding the steamer together and that old quartermaster gave me the rifle and the Colt, and the papers to go with them. He told me I might need them to shoot buffalo and rattlesnakes out West. I told him that deer and copperheads would be the critters in my sights. Said that I had saved his ass from a court marshal, and that Colonel Roosevelt had personally thanked him for shoeing the horse. And ya' know, Roosevelt took that gelding back on the steamer with him and gave it to his little boys. The newspapers made a big deal about it."

Cody picked up the Colt and looked a little puzzled.

"This thing's too long for a four-and-a-half-inch barrel and too short for a seven-and-a-half-inch barrel. What gives?"

"It's five-inch and that's how the Army wanted 'em," Chet said. "When you're dealin' with the army, you just do what they say. They never told us why on anything."

GETTING BACK TO THE ROUTINE

For the next week or so Byron and Helen told everyone to let Chet rest, that there would be some readjustment now that he was back to civilian life. With Pops' bad hip, Cody really needed help on the farm, but he followed his parents' orders. His only help for the heavy work was George Timmons. George was a nice fellow, about thirty years old, but as Pops always said, "That boy's one egg shy of a dozen." Nobody knew for sure, but many thought George must have been kicked in the head by a horse as a boy. It didn't mean he hadn't any talents. When it came to horses, George could handle them as well as Cody and Chet. He also had no trouble cutting hay while using the farm's McCormick-Deering sickle mower that was pulled by one of the work mules. He was equally talented at using the buck rake after the hay had time to dry in the fields. He'd try about anything he was asked to do. If it was something new it took him a while to think about it. Other things could end up being a nightmare.

For example, Chet and Cody made a good team when it came to making haystacks in the summer. They'd lay down eight-foot hedge posts. Chet would throw the hay down from the wagon to Cody using a pitchfork in just the right way. Cody would start to build a pyramid of hay with his pitchfork. With the exception of the bottom of the stack, every forkful of hay helped build a narrower stack as it was piled on. The purpose being that a cone-shaped pile, with the point on top, would help rain run off the haystack and keep the forage from getting damp inside and rotting.

As much as George tried, he just couldn't get the hang of throwing the hay down the same way Chet did. The result was that it took poor Cody twice as long to get a haystack built. He tried not to lose his temper. George was a hard worker and, unfortunately, got picked on by way too many people in the area. Some of them were the teenagers that hung around Mr. Frost's place.

Meanwhile, Chet was getting used to being back home. He'd rise early as the mourning doves began to coo, have a cup of coffee, and sit on the front porch as the sun came up and painted the fields a shade of golden yellow. For him, the farm was a site for sore eyes—and one of the best spreads in Jefferson County. Across the dirt entry road was one of the largest sycamore trees in the county and a creek bed that only ran in the spring, which, during heavy rains, separated the house from the big unpainted oak barn where Pops kept the stallions. Rex was a four-year-old that was seal black in color whose only distinctive mark was a white snip on his nose. He was tall for a Morgan, about fifteen hands high. Monty was a seven-year-old dun with a white blaze with three out of four of the legs having white anklets. Then there was Samson, a six-year-old black and brown-colored Mammoth jack that had been a real plus in fathering quality mules with the Harbison brood mares, and with mares brought in by farmers from miles around. He was almost as tall as Red. All three had stalls made of extra-thick cuts of oak that went up nearly to the beams in the barn. And each had their own paddock made with railings just as high as those in the stalls.

Another large paddock with tall railings was attached to the east side of the barn. That's where the breeding took place unless it was requested that one of the stallions be taken to another farm where numerous mares and fillies were waiting.

Just east of the barn were the remains of the old cabin that Grandpa had for two slaves who had worked the farm before the War Between the States. Further east was the springhouse where Ma and Lize kept milk, cream and butter cool. In the warmer weather, the men would fetch the supplies from the springhouse. It was a haven for copperhead snakes.

Although Chet had been forbidden to help Cody, the young man worked harder than he should, mainly with Red. It became a daily routine for Chet to greet the big gelding shortly after breakfast. First Chet would say a kind word, and then lift each of the horse's hooves to clean them, always using a gentle hand. Then he would brush the animal down, being very careful when he went along the horse's belly. It made Red very skittish until he became used to it. When Red was farther out in the pasture Chet would walk half the distance, always with a carrot, an apple or a sugar cube in his hand. Then, he'd put two fingers in his mouth and whistle and Red would come running. After saddling up, the two went for long rides. Chet made him go over wooden bridges and sometimes he'd drag a sack tied to a rope alongside the horse. Backing up and tight left and right turns were all part of training to make Red a dependable partner on the farm. He'd even jumped the animal over some of the smaller creek beds that were scattered throughout the farm. Red's reactions and responses improved as he became more accustomed to the routines.

Later Chet started firing a .22 from a distance, getting closer and closer as Red got accustomed to the report. It was a slow process. He would tie Red up to a railing by the stud barn and then practice shooting at the rusted tin cans that were dumped into the creek bed quite a distance away. The first few times a shot was fired the tall gelding jumped backwards and almost broke the reins loose. Although Red got calmer, his ears continued to flip back anytime he heard a firearm go off. After a while it didn't matter if Chet was using his .22 revolver he got as a Christmas present when he was ten years old or the .45 he brought back from Cuba, the horse made a steady improvement, except his ears continued to show his dislike for gunfire. His ears fluttered back and forth each time a shot was fired. Chet seldom missed and he could keep a can jumping in the air until all five rounds were spent.

One day as he was walking Red back to his stall Chet stopped to say hello to Callie who was now helping with the chores by hanging wash out on the line.

Callie began to feel like family with the Harbisons. She talked a little more than before, but often only about the weather or what the preacher had said at church on Sunday. She only spoke about her parents when asked. And while her nightmares were fewer, there were still times when Helen would rush into her room during the middle of the night and wake her to stop the crying and screams.

Despite being a city girl Callie was a quick study when it came to handling chores she had never been asked to perform at her parents' house—those were for the maid, Agnus. But being from the city she had lots of questions to ask and everyone from Mr. Harbison down to Lize was patient when explaining things to her. Beth was becoming a big sister of sorts. Most important, Callie began to smile more, which made her attractive five-foot, three-inch petite figure even more noticeable.

"Why did you buy a horse that was in such sad shape when your folks had all of these healthy animals on the farm?" she asked as Chet greeted her.

Chet tried not to stare at the pretty face as he spoke.

"I rode the streets of New York in a buggy with my friend Ritchie seeing the sites for more than a week, and part of what I saw I didn't like," Chet said as he petted the side of Red's neck. "Peddlers and teamsters fed their horses barely enough to survive and then worked them beyond what a healthy animal could do. And when they couldn't work anymore they'd unharness them and let them die in the streets. The stench was unbelievable. Ritchie told me that the 'dead wagon' picked up more than a hundred horses a week to process their hides and sell their meat for dog food. You wouldn't believe the number of sick and skin-and-bone nags barely being able to walk that were hitched to wagons and carts. I didn't want that to happen to this one, and he was headed in that direction with the type of owner he had."

Callie recognized that Chet wasn't the same boy he was before he left for the war. *He used to have a devilish grin on his face almost anytime I saw him and he always smiled at me. Before he left he and his friend, Pete McKinney, had always been joking around and stirring up innocent trouble, some of which had made Father furious*, she thought. *Now he hardly ever smiles.*

About two years earlier one of her father's prized Angus heifers disappeared and Cavanaugh was going around accusing everyone of stealing it. Wheeler Frost mentioned that no calves had been missing from anyone since "Ol' Three Toes" had left the country more than a year earlier. Callie had learned that Three Toes was a cougar that wandered into Jefferson County and terrorized farmers to the point where they wouldn't let their children go out alone. Hunting parties were organized and traps were set, but the only thing they ever caught was one toe of the big cat. He left his distinguished paw print behind at every carcass the farmers found—and then he disappeared.

Cavanaugh demanded that those same farmers help him hunt down this deadly animal, even though no one had seen hide nor hair of it—at least not until Chet and Pete got wind of Cavanaugh's demands.

The two got together behind the McKinney barn and carved paw prints using soft white pine that was easy to cut with their Barlow knives. For two solid weeks the two hooligans tramped all over the area with the rear paws tied to the soles of Chet's boots and the fronts, one with a missing toe, tied to Pete's.

Callie remembered her father ordering all of his hands to keep rifles with them at all times. If they didn't own one he bought one for them from Mr. Frost. Every time a chicken disappeared or a cow or a horse got through a fence it was blamed on Three Toes.

Chet and Pete were having the time of their lives leaving prints nearly everywhere they went, and both continued to start rumors about the cougar, that is until Pete's father found the wooden paws hidden under a feed bin in his barn. Pete "got his hide tanned," he later bragged, as did Chet. The two co-conspirators took their beatings as a badge of honor, but apologizing to the entire town in front of the general store, especially to Mr. Cavanaugh, wasn't part of their glory. Both were embarrassed and had a hard time looking into the eyes of the men who had stayed up nights trying to kill an animal that was nowhere to be found.

Callie was near Mr. Frost and Mr. Harbison when the apologies were made, and she heard Mr. Harbison whisper into the shopkeeper's ear. "I really hated takin' that young'un of mine to the woodshed," he said. "Fact of the matter is, I wish I had thought up the idea myself just to get the hair up on Cavanaugh's backside."

Callie had to force herself from giggling at the comment, but she knew just what Mr. Harbison was talking about. It was funny that the boys had made a fool out of her egotistical father. And, as it had turned out, the lost heifer had gotten through the fence to the Jones' place. The farmer, or one of his sons, likely pushed it back through his tattered fence line when he learned the hunting parties were coming his way.

The punishment wasn't over yet for the two boys. They agreed to clean Cavanaugh's barn every week for a month for all the grief they had caused. Cavanaugh, who had only kept his matched carriage sorrels and a milk cow in the barn, invited all of his hired hands to keep their horses inside even though it was common practice to let them graze in the pasture when not being put to work. As the boys shoveled shit into the manure spreader, Cavanaugh watched every move they made. One day Pete got a splinter in his hand and headed toward a supply box in the barn to look for a pair of gloves. Cavanaugh blocked Pete's path with his wide girth, and then planted himself on top of the box, refusing to move. He was a vindictive man to say the least who was always trying to make himself look more important than others.

CALLIE

Callie was a shy but inquisitive girl with no experience about farm life. Her mother and father had sheltered her once they moved to Grubville a few years earlier. Her mother taught her to play a baby grand piano when she was a small girl and bookshelves at their farmhouse had included the works of Shakespeare and Mark Twain alike. She knew nothing of life on a horse ranch or a cattle farm. Neighbors soon discovered that her father knew very little as well. He had bought too many cows for the amount of pasture on his land. With him dead, the Harbisons had made an attempt to keep them fed by moving part of the herd to their land. But in reality the herd had to be cut back. Winter was nearing and calves were coming on in the spring. Because of all the legalities of it, Cohen Lee, the Rural Free Delivery mail carrier, had advised Pops to visit the county seat in Hillsboro to get power of attorney to make sure no one tried to take advantage of what was now Callie's property. She had informed the Harbisons that "Mother and Father" had no other living relatives.

Callie knew very little about the fire that had taken her parents' lives. She had already gone to sleep that night and only remembered hearing shouting and smelling smoke when she awoke. Her bedroom was engulfed in flames. Jumping out of the window as flames singed her hair and nightgown, the teenager barely made it out of the farmhouse alive. One of the few questions she asked that related to the tragedy was when Helen awakened her during one of her nightmares. "Was I saying anything important that would explain the fire?" she asked.

"No dear," Helen said. "You've got to quit worrying about that. We will probably never know."

Callie also thought a lot about the young soldier who had returned home. Even with all the home cooking, he didn't look well, and she had heard Lize say how "Chester" seemed to be having numerous nightmares as well. Thunder and lightning during heavy rainstorms brought them out, Lize said. It worried the old woman whenever she heard his screams on a restless night. Her bedroom was just down the hall form his.

One day while Callie was peeling potatoes with Lize for the noon dinner she asked the dark-skinned woman why Chet had ever left the farm to fight in a war in a foreign land.

"Lordy child, that's a good question that everyone asked after they got his letter," Lize said as she reached for another potato. "But I know most of it. Poor Chester was having a bad time of it here. He had been head over heals over that Simpson girl up the road. I never liked that girl, thought she was kinda' trashy, but Chester, he thought she was everything."

Lize was not one to stop talking once she was asked a question. She had a lot of opinions just waiting to be told and she knew that most adults didn't want to hear them. She continued as she dumped the potato peelings into a bucket for the two hogs that were kept farther down the creek. "He proposed to that hussy and plans were in the makin' for a big wedding. A month before the big day, she left town with a slicked-up travelin' man who sold pots and pans. Said he was rich and she could live a life of leisure in some big city. I knew that man was no good too. Mizzez Helen bought some of those pots and they started rustin' within a week. Poor Chester's big heart was broken. Then, Cody and Beth announced their marriage plans just after that. Cody don't own no land so Chester had to move out of the room he shared with his brother and move into that little room by the hall. He said he didn't mind, but he had planned on the bigger room for him and his own bride."

Then the subject changed.

"And I used to think Chet and Cody were noise makers growin' up in that bedroom across from mine," Lize said. "It was nothing compared to all the noise that Cody and Mizzez Beth makes in there. She's a giglin' girl, makin' all types of sounds when she and Cody come up to 'sleep.' I betcha' Mr. Byron and Mizzez Helen don't get much sleep anymore either with their bedroom just below. Now they got that little baby up there too, and sometimes they bring him in by me when they needs their 'privacy.'"

Callie started to blush but she didn't try to stop the woman from continuing. She just soaked it all in.

"Anyway, a couple of weeks later, Chester was on his way to deliver some horses to Rolla for his daddy," Lize said. "He didn't take his own horse, just rode one of 'em they were sellin'. A week later, a freighter dropped off his saddle and a bank draft for the horses at Mr. Frost's place with a note sayin' Chester had gone on to San Antonio to join the Rough Riders. I cried and cried thinkin' that child would never make it back home."

Old Lize began to tear up as she finally finished her talk.

Another source for Callie was Beth. They were almost the same age and Beth had taken the city girl under her wings, the same way Helen and Lize had. While they taught the girl how to sew, Beth was doing her best to get Callie out in the real world instead of staying cooped up in the farmhouse. Helen had told Callie she could play the old pump organ in the parlor anytime she wanted and that's where she stayed most of the time unless she was asked to do chores. The Harbisons had heard Callie playing her family's piano up on the hill during warm weather when the windows were open. Now they could hear the organ even louder when they were doing chores throughout the day. With the leaves starting to turn and the temperature cooler Beth had asked Callie if she wanted to go horseback riding to check the mares in the west pasture up on the hill.

"Mother and Father always said it was unladylike to ride horseback, that a carriage was more appropriate," she explained. "I've never ridden a horse before."

"You're not in Kansas City anymore, girl," Beth said. "If you want to see things you've got to get in a saddle. You can't be awaitin' for someone to hitch up a buggy, and a buggy won't go a lot of places where a saddle horse can go.

I've been riding since I was a girl on my daddy's Belgium farm."

Callie didn't know what a "Belgium farm" was and wondered if Beth's father lived in Europe. Beth finally convinced Callie that riding in a saddle was now acceptable.

"Look, if for no other reason, you've got to be able to go out in the fields and inspect those cows of yours. They're really your responsibility and you need to learn as much as you can about them. It's going to be your livelihood," Beth said.

The next time they went to town in the buggy, the two went shopping for a pair of blue jeans at the general store. Callie sorted through the folded jeans and retrieved a size six. Then she went behind the curtain in the back of the store and tried them on.

"I think these will work," she said as she showed them to Beth. They were several sizes smaller than what Beth wore herself. But Callie's newfound older sister was not pleased with the baggy fit.

"They're too loose," Beth said. They're going to, uh, get caught up in the tall brush. Try these fours."

When Callie returned the second time, Beth had a smile on her face. The jeans fit snug around Callie's narrow waist and hips, accentuating her features.

"Well, Okay," Callie answered, concerned that they were too tight, as she looked at the lower half of her body.

Beth paid for the jeans with her egg money and then it was time to go home and learn to ride.

Maybe some of the boys—maybe even Chet—will start to notice Callie, Beth thought. She had no idea that Chet and Callie already had noticed a lot of each other the morning after he had returned home.

Beth had a chestnut Morgan filly that Cody had given her for a wedding present, and Callie was to ride "Momma Helen's" buckskin gelding, appropriately called "Buck."

"This horse seems to be very gentle," Callie said. "And from what I've seen so far, he's not in a big rush to get somewhere." Meanwhile, she watched Beth keep a tight rein or her three-year-old, a horse with quite a bit more spirit.

"Buck is about 10 years old and it's almost impossible to get him into a dead run," Beth said. "He's not a Morgan like most of the horses on the farm and nobody really knows what breed he is. Momma Helen rescued him several years ago from a farmer who said he had no hay to feed it during one of the worst winters the county had seen in decades. The farmer didn't have much for himself and his family to eat either, so Momma Helen traded four slabs of bacon and a big sack of black beans for the horse. She gave him some flour too so they could have bread and biscuits. Turns out Buck was trained for harness and saddle, and had a really smooth gate. Pops calls it single-footing. He can pull a buggy or plow a field, and he's got a real easy feel when you ride him."

Because of the horse's slow pace and calm demeanor, Beth determined that Buck was the best horse for a beginner like Callie. There wasn't any chance of the horse getting

Callie hurt. With just a few instructions on reining, Callie was ready to ride.

Their first stop was the family cemetery up in the west pasture where Callie's parents were buried. If only she could remember more about that night. There were strange voices and shouting when she awoke, along with her father's ranting. It was all hazy. She couldn't remember details.

A month passed since Cody placed the hand-made wooden caskets of her parents and their maid in back of the hay wagon and had a team of mules pull it up the rocky path through the woods to the pasture—all while the rain poured on the mourners. Pops, Helen and Callie followed in the family buggy. Behind them was the preacher and many of the families who lived nearby.

Today, with fall in the air, there were no fresh flowers to put on the graves, but Helen had helped Callie make a pretty bow that could be placed between the headstones when the two girls made the ride up the hill to give their respects. There was a moment or two of silence and Callie wiped a tear from her eye.

"I guess I'm ready," she said. "Where do we go from here?"

With that Beth gave a guided tour of the farm, visiting five major pastures that were separated by woods. Then they rode back to the Cavanaugh farm to inspect the herd. Neither girl said a word as they rode past what remained of Callie's former home. The only parts left were a few of the charred beams near what used to be the front porch. Callie nudged

Buck to pick up his pace up the hill to where the cattle were grazing.

"Why does that cow look so different from the others?" Callie asked while pointing to the biggest animal in the herd.

Beth tried not to grin. "That's the daddy," she said. He's a bull and all the others are momma cows," she said.

From then on there were daily rides. Together, Callie and Beth delivered eggs to the general store, cleaned up the schoolhouse for church services and stopped by Mr. Frost's to see if there had been any exciting phone calls from the city. Mr. Nelson at the general store even started to save the crumpled newspapers that came packed with supplies for the store. Callie read every one of them. Most came from St. Louis or Kansas City, but sometimes she would find one from Denver, Chicago or even New York. She loved to read the news from the big cities, even if it was several weeks or months old.

The only time she put a paper down before finishing it was when she saw a two-paragraph article in the St. Louis paper about her parents being killed. It surprised her that a big city newspaper would even cover the event. She continued to find the newspapers interesting, but inside hoped there were no more articles about the fire. Besides, there wasn't much to read at the Harbison home—the Holy Bible, the Sears & Roebuck and Montgomery Ward catalogs, and Pops' magazines on animal husbandry that included his favorite, *Breeder's Gazette and American Stock Farm.*

As time passed, just as Beth expected, the teenage males around town, and even some of the older men, began to take a second look at the redheaded teenage girl who had often been thought of as "that stuck-up skinny kid from the city." Callie, however, paid them little mind other than a pleasant "Hello."

FARM WORK

Chet continued to have good days and bad days and he began cutting back on the tree bark that he chewed on. There wasn't much left by now. He had put on a little weight, as did Red. His morning routine would continue much as it did after he first returned home. After breakfast, he would grab an apple or just a sugar cube and walk to the middle of the pasture where Red was kept. Then he'd put two fingers between his teeth and whistle. Red would come running for his morning treat. After the snack was devoured Chet hoisted himself onto the tall horse's back, grabbed a handful of mane and let the horse take him back to the main gate near the house.

Chet felt good enough to work for his keep and the first chore was to bring about fifteen head of the Cavanaugh Angus cattle to the river bottom forty acres of the Harbison farm. Cody was gentling a two-year old liver-colored Morgan filly while Chet continued his training of the long-legged gelding that he rescued from St. Louis. With the help of Pebbles, the black cows moved at a constant pace as Cody and Chet passed the burned out Cavanaugh home.

"Was there much left of the bodies when you found them?" Chet asked.

"They were burnt to a crisp," Cody said. "I'd never seen anything like it. It was like picking up charred lumber when I loaded them in the wagon. But what was really strange is how me and Pops found them. They were on the floor of what used to be the parlor and they were all right next to each other. It didn't seem right for a fire that might have started from a lit cigar ash or even an oil lamp that fell over. It looked like the heaviest part of the fire was right by them.

"Maybe the three were all trying to put out the fire?"

"Maybe," Cody said. "But it still didn't look right. Pops called the Sheriff's office from Mr. Frost's store, but they said it wasn't worth the bother to come and take a look—farm houses burn down all the time from lightning or someone just being careless."

Callie had agreed with Pops to sell the two carriage horses and Mr. Lee was looking for someone who appreciated fine animals. Cody and Chet decided to leave the bull with the remaining thirty-five cows still grazing at Cavanaugh's'. All appeared to be bred and there was no need to bring a bull onto Harbison property. Keeping two Morgan stallions and one Mammoth jack provided plenty of work for Chet, Cody, and even George. After the cows were rounded up it was time to get back to their own work. Close to twenty Harbison mares needed to be bred before winter and there were ranchers from as far as Catawissa who would be bring their mares to the farm as well.

And then there was Mr. Lee. Although he was the area's RFD mail carrier he was also a salesman who bought and sold anything he could along his route, including horses. If he had mares in season, he would have Cody or Chet bring Rex or Monty over to "do their chores." Any mare he sold would bring more money when she was bred to a Harbison stallion. Although most brought their mares to Harbisons', Mr. Lee's was the exception. He always had plenty to trade for stud services and they would bring Rex or Monty to him. In fact, after a series of visits Rex didn't have to be led by a horse and rider. He would usually try to lead the charge once they turned off the main route and onto Booger Mountain Road where Mr. Lee lived. Rex was a male who loved his job.

Samson the Mammoth jack was "put to work" the next day after Cody and Chet picked out three mares ready to be bred.

Beth and Callie were pulling turnips from behind the wire fence across the creek as Cody and Chet brought two mares up to the paddock. Samson, in his own private paddock was pacing back and forth, raising his head as high as he could, braying at the top of his lungs.

"What's going on over there?" Callie asked Beth.

"It's breeding time and Samson is about to help make some baby mules," she said, knowing she would get Callie's attention.

"But don't mules make mules? Callie asked.

"No, it don't work like that," Beth said. "Mares and Jacks make 'em. Mules will try their darndest but it just don't work.

60

Now some folks will breed a Jenny—that's the momma donkey—with a stallion, but they don't look the same as a mule. They call 'em hinnies.

"Come on, I want to show you the new kittens over in the hayloft—and a couple other things of interest to a city gal," she quipped.

Chet, Cody, and George didn't notice the girls crossing the creek and entering the backside of the barn, and Beth didn't try to get their attention. Once they entered the barn Callie smelled a familiar smell, that of Mentholatum. Susan Cavanaugh had rubbed it on her daughter's chest and feet as a child, anytime she had a bad cold.

"Why am I smelling that smell?" Callie asked.

"That's because George just put Mentholatum in Rex's and Monty's nostrils," Beth said. "It's not their time to be doin' the daddying so now they can't smell the mares like Samson can."

The two young women climbed the ladder to the loft to view the new batch of kittens. The old gray farm cat had never been touched by a human. She hissed and ran off, leaving the kittens to the two girls. Beth, with the help of Callie, grabbed a couple of the kittens and found a place to sit in the hay near the opening of the loft door. A bay mare was in the paddock and George opened the gate to let Samson in.

"Boy, oh boy does he have any easy job," George shouted to Chet and Cody. The brothers just grinned. George was like a twelve-year old whenever breeding took place. Even at thirty, to their knowledge, he had never been with a woman.

Beth got a chuckle seeing Callie watch what was going on below in the paddock. Samson pranced around in an excited state, but when he approached the mare, she kicked as hard as she could with both rear hooves. The three men all jumped back as a natural reaction, and then laughed. Samson continued with his conquest, raising his nose as high as he could, braying to the top of his lungs.

"I hear tell in the city that some of these horse breeders actually hobble the mare up so she can't kick the stallion," Chet said.

"I suppose that might be a good idea," Cody said," but Samson only needed to be kicked once in the 'cookies' and he knows how to wait it out."

Callie's full attention was on the paddock, in particular at Samson. The mare circled around several times with Samson following, but staying a safe distance away until she was ready.

"She doesn't want anything to do with him," Callie said.

"It's just like boys," Beth said. "You don't want to kiss them right away until they've sweet talked you and danced with you a little bit. You'll see."

After urinating several times, the mare finally relaxed her rear legs into a slight squat and lifted her tail. Samson knew it was time and mounted the mare. It was over in less than 20 seconds.

Callie's face became beet red and her mouth hung wide open.

"Oh my gosh. Samson is big—all over," she whispered.

"Well that's true but he's not as 'big' as my daddy's Belgium draft horse stallion," Beth bragged.

"What's the stallion's name," Callie asked.

"Goliath," Beth said.

Both women couldn't hold back. They were giggling like a couple of schoolgirls. They held their hands over their mouths but it was too late. Chet and Cody heard them.

"What are you two doing up there?" Cody asked.

"Just lookin' at the new kitty cats," Beth said. "What are you doing down there? She could hardly keep a straight face.

Cody gave Chet a big grin. "Come on little brother. Let's turn this gal out and bring another one in. It won't take Samson long to get ready for a new girlfriend."

George scratched his head, somewhat confused, as he watched the two women exit the barn and cross the creek heading toward the white clapboard farmhouse.

"What are you two girls doing over by that barn?" Lize asked. "That's man's work goin' on over there. You two should be ashamed of yourselves. I got a notion to tell your momma on you Mizzez Beth. You don't go over by them animals when the men are a-workin'. If you need somethin' to do we got plenty of pumpkins and squash to can."

The two cohorts, now as thick as thieves, couldn't stop laughing. It was feeding time for little Cody who was starting to whine. Once they reached the kitchen, Helen handed the baby off to Beth as the two young women headed toward the parlor. Callie had finally gotten used to Beth nursing the baby in front of her even though she felt a bit uncomfortable. On the other hand, she always enjoyed talking with and learning from Beth. And after her visit to the hayloft, Callie began to take more interest in reading Mr. Harbison's stack of farm journals. After all, she owned plenty of cattle.

Lize continued to rant after the girls left the kitchen, even though Helen acted as though she knew nothing about what had just happened. Pops walked into the kitchen just in time to hear Lize continue about girls "stayin' away from men's work." He knocked his pipe along the wooden counter, refilled it with tobacco, but hesitated to light it with all the noise going on.

"What in tarnation just happened?" he asked.

Helen, who was washing dishes at the sink, turned to him and put her hands on her hips.

"Nothing important, 'cept it appears Beth is helping Cassie learn about farm work—and growing up."

"What's wrong with that?" Then he sucked on the pipe, putting the lit match to the bowl. "We need all the help we can get around this place. Winter will be here soon and we ain't nearly ready with everything that's happening around here. We're going to have to help that girl sell some of these cows before winter hits. Nobody's goin' ta wanta buy them after the first snow falls.

Helen grinned, threw the dishtowel at her husband and walked away. "I'll tell you all about it later," she said.

TROUBLE AT WHEELER'S

Winter was on the way and with Chet feeling better he began to challenge himself on how much he could do. There was plenty of wood to cut and with the help of George, the two brothers began to spend at least two or three hours every afternoon sawing and splitting logs from the timbers that had been cut during the summer. It wasn't hard to get up a sweat even with the colder temperatures in the early morning and late afternoon.

"We've been stackin' wood for quite a spell now," Chet said as he wiped the sweat off of his brow. I'm beat. Supper won't be ready for another hour or so. Do you want to grab a draft up at Mr. Frost's?"

"No, you go ahead," Cody said. "Beth wants to show me the dress she and Lize been workin' on for the dance up at the sale barn next week. Callie's makin' one too and I guess I'm supposed to look at 'em and tell them how pretty they look. You know how it is—she'd look good in rags but I got to say it with the dress on her."

Chet walked down to the pasture gate and whistled. Within minutes Chief Red Man was standing at the fence and ready to be saddled. A carrot was waiting for the steed.

Although still tall and slender, Red was starting to fill out and looked healthy and strong. For some reason he still didn't look like much of a horse until he was under saddle though. When that happened he bowed his neck and his ears perked up at attention. He was a beautiful animal that took pleasure in pleasing his new master. And why not? He had never been treated so well in his entire life.

Ten minutes later Chet was walking into Mr. Frost's store.

"Hi, I guess I'd like one of those new Falstaffs," Chet said.

"Son, you go help yourself, and if you don't mind, could you keep an eye on things for me? I have to go back to the barn and check an order that just came in."

"Sure enough, Mr. Frost. It doesn't look like you will be very busy. I didn't see anyone on the way in."

Chet helped himself to mug of beer from the tap, blew the foam off the top and found a stool to sit on at the bar. He was ready to relax. It had been a hard day.

Then it happened—the three older Spragg boys scuffled into the store with one thing in mind. Chet could smell the body odor when they walked in. None of them believed in bathing often, or in washing their clothes for that matter. The Spraggs were known for stealing hogs from wherever they could find them and they never bothered to wash off the hog-slop evidence once the deed was done.

"Embarrass me in front of my little brother, will you," Albert Spragg said. He appeared much braver with his older brothers in tow.

Chet knew it wouldn't pay to wait and see what happened next. He jumped to his feet and ran full force into Dutch Spragg, the oldest and the biggest of the trio. His hand-to-hand combat experience in Cuba would be his only chance to survive the brawl. Within seconds, Dutch was falling backwards over a table and then landed flat on his back on the floor. Chet jumped on top of him and began pounding punch after punch into his face. Finally after some hesitation, Luke and Albert joined in and pulled the Rough Rider to his feet, both gripping onto his arms and shoulders as possible. Dutch painfully rose to his feet and wiped the blood flowing from his split lip and bloody nose. Raising his left arm, he punched Chet in the face as hard as he could and then decided to lower his aim for his next blow. Chet didn't have a chance but he tried his best, lifting his leg and kicking Dutch in the stomach. But that was all he could muster. Dutch's two brothers held him tight and watched as Dutch continued to pound the Harbison boy with blows to his chest and stomach.

Within a minute or two of the brawl starting Chet looked up to see Pete McKinney bounding into the store and lock his right elbow around Dutch's neck. Out of the blue, the odds had changed—but not by much. Pete McKinney was the scrawniest teenager in the county. Dripping wet he weighed in at a hundred and ten pounds and at best, his height only reached the top of Dutch's shoulders. The funny thing was that Pete never seemed to notice how short and skinny he was. If there was a fight, he'd never stand and watch. He had to be a part of it. There was never a hesitation in entering into a brawl when his best friend was on the shit end of the stick.

Dutch Spragg whirled his body around in a circle trying to free himself from Pete's grip, but it was to no avail. The more he whirled the tighter Pete squeezed his arm around Dutch's throat.

The change in the odds gave Chet just enough time to break free of Albert and Luke. Chet elbowed Albert in the gut as hard as he could and then threw a wild punch that grazed Luke's jaw just enough to knock him off balance.

Dutch whirled in a circle as fast as he could, freeing himself of the newcomer as Pete flew into a stack of burlap feed bags stacked against the wall. Cracked corn began to spill on the floor. Almost losing his balance from the kernels on the floor, Dutch managed to grab Pete by the collar and pulled back his fist, planning to finish the "little runt" off when all five men heard the distinct racking of a pump shotgun.

Wheeler Frost's lean silhouette could be seen in the opening of the back door and his Model 97 Winchester 12-guage had a bead on Dutch Spragg.

"You can get on those nags of yours and head out of town or spend the night locked in my cellar with the rats until a deputy sheriff gets here in the morning—it's your choice." The old man stayed as cool as a cucumber as he continued to level the shotgun at the tallest of the Spragg boys.

The Spraggs walked to the front door like dogs with their tails between their legs. The odds were no longer in their favor, and they knew that the former Confederate sergeant wasn't afraid to pull the trigger. The stories about Wheeler's battles against the Yankees may have been stretched over the years, but nobody doubted that he had done his share of killing in his younger days.

Pete limped over to the store's entrance, pushed the front screen door open and walked outside as the riders headed back to the main road that would take them to their Big River shack. Soon the sounds of hooves became more faint.

"Two of those stump jumpers were on their regular plugs, but Dutch is ridin' a high-steppin' pinto with a fancy Mexican saddle," Pete said as he brushed the feed dust off of his clothes. His shirt was torn and his lip was bleeding as he smiled and looked at Chet. He bent down and picked up Chet's crushed army hat off the floor and then sailed it through the air toward his best friend. Chet reached up with one leg off the ground and caught it.

"Just the same old story with you Harbison," Pete said. "It's a good thing I happened by to save your ass, just like I've been doin' since we were kids."

"Save me?" Chet said. "I could have whipped those bottom feeders with one hand tied behind my back! You had a tiger by the tail when you latched onto Dutch Spragg. If he'd a thrown you up against a wall instead of those feed sacks, he'd a flattened you like a pancake."

"Fat chance in hell that would ever happen," Pete said. "You're about the poorest excuse for a scruffler that I've ever seen. I heard you were back in town—just got back from Cuba myself—you know—that little town near St. Clair."

Wheeler stood with his hands on his hips watching the two boys try to out-do the other, just as he had the entire time they were growing up. By now, both young men were laughing so hard it hurt. Chet showed no noticeable cuts or bruises but he was holding his side with his right hand. Neither admitted to having any pain.

The two talked old times over more than a beer or two after they had helped Mr. Frost clean up the spilled grain. Then, Chet looked at his pocket watch and saw it was suppertime.

"Why don't you come and eat with us?" Chet asked.

"Maybe another time. There's gal sweet on me over in Dittmer and her momma's goin' have a meal ready for us by the time I can get there.

The two thanked Mr. Frost for his rescue and walked out the door. As they did, Chet saw a familiar face leaving the general store across the street. It was Lori Simpson—at least that was her name when she left town with the peddler.

"Oh Chet, I'm so glad to see you made it back," she said as she rushed up to greet him. Lori was wearing a white store-bought dress from the city. Like other outfits she had worn, this one gave every man a view of her large chest. Dropping her parasol to the ground, she ran up to Chet and wrapped her arms around him, kissing him on the lips.

Chet's shoulders stiffened and he tried to step back and break away.

"I just got back in town, too," she said as she gripped his hands with hers. I've got so much to tell you about our plans now that you're back. I missed you so much. You know I'm single again. Actually I never really married. Daddy had the marriage annulled, so it really didn't count. I just can't wait to 'get together' with you again."

"It's been a long time," Chet said matter-of-factly. He stepped back several feet and placed his attention on Red as she tried to approach him once more.

Pete McKinney glared at the young woman. He didn't want to see his best friend get hurt again. But then again, Lori wasn't hard on a man's eyes.

That gal's got the longest legs on a woman I've ever seen—legs all the way to heaven, Pete thought.

She's nearly as tall as Chet and that figure of hers, you just don't see someone like that that shows it off as much as she does. Wouldn't surprise me if she had to have someone put heavy-duty thread on those buttons up by her chest to keep them from bustin' out. That material up thar is tighter than my momma's girdle. That's about as far as I can compliment a bitch like her.

Pete stepped in. "Come on Chet, I decided I do want to eat with you and your folks, and we're runnin' late."

Lori scowled at Pete as he tipped his hat to her and ushered Chet and Red further away from her. Lori did an about-face and sauntered over to the buggy where her father sat waiting for her. He had already picked up her umbrella and had witnessed the whole ordeal. He said nothing, but smiled at his daughter as she joined him on the carriage seat.

The ride back was a bit uncomfortable for Chet, but with Red's easy gait the short distance was bearable. Besides, Chet wouldn't be able to say how bad he hurt if he wanted to— Pete talked the whole way—about the jobs he'd had, the women he'd been with and the battles he'd had with some of the biggest brutes in the county. Chet believed none of it, but always enjoyed a good story from his best friend.

Chicken and dumplings were the main course at the supper table. But it was Pete who got most of the attention as he kept on rambling about how he had saved Chet—one more time—and that Mr. Frost had helped a little as well. Everyone was used to Pete's braggin' but Lize kept rolling her eyes every time the skinny runt of a neighbor went to the next scenario. She also managed get up from her table to slap his hand as he placed second and third helpings of chicken and dumplings onto his plate—for someone his size, he could sure put down the food.

"Let him have all he wants Lize," Chet said. "He can't talk as much when his mouth is full!"

Then the subject changed. "Can you imagine the gall of that Lori Simpson, coming up to Chet outside of Mr. Frost's and givin' him a hug like a momma grizzly bear? That woman..."

Pete, jumped back in his seat as he felt a sharp kick from across the table and a cold stare from Beth.

"That woman..."

This time the kick was harder, and right at his shin. He finally got the point.

"Ya know Miss Lize, no one makes better chicken and dumplings than you!

Now Helen Harbison was giving him a cold stare. "Pete, Lize wrung the chicken's neck but I'm the one that made this here supper."

"Yes'm, just as I was sayin', nobody makes better meals than you two." Then he changed the subject. "I went up to Cuba for a barn raisin' job—you all know how good I am at that. And I was plannin' on comin' back home when I heard the Frisco was hirin' gandy dancers. Those folks worked us 14 hours a day and gave us plenty of food, but it wasn't nothing like the fine cookin' all the woman folk here make. I just about wasted away because it was so bad."

Almost everyone turned to look at the same scrawny body they'd seen since he was five years old. And sure enough, Pete was reaching for more green beans.

"Did you and Lize make pies today as well?"

Half of those seated at the table were rolling their eyes as Pete tried to get himself out of the corner he had painted himself in; Callie remained silent. Instead she kept her eyes on Chet. It seemed to be the first time since his return that he was really enjoying life. He was smiling—and laughing every time his old friend Pete put his foot in his mouth or when Lize slapped Cody's hand when he attempted to take too big of a portion from the bowls in the center of the table. *...ting to be that devilish fun-loving boy I used to kn(went away to war*, she thought. And that made wanting to spend more time with him.

Chet didn't notice her stares, but two others did—Beth, who thought they would make a perfect couple, and Helen Harbison who worried for her son, who had been through so much in the past year. She didn't want him to get hurt, and she also didn't want things to get out of hand since he and Callie were under the same roof.

LIZE WILSON

Lize, the former slave, had also become one of Callie's confidants but the old woman, who was in her sixties, never talked about her past. And it made Callie all the more curious about the colored woman. Lize had her own large bedroom upstairs, but sat at a separate small table in the kitchen during meals. Still, she seemed to play a major part in the Harbison family. She took pride in making everyone—even Byron and Helen—toe the mark if it involved something important.

With breakfast finished on a Tuesday morning, Callie found herself sitting at the kitchen table with Byron Harbison.

"Callie, now that I've been appointed what the courts call your 'guardian' there are some decisions that are going to have to be made. Since you're almost full growed you need to be a part of it. Your pa had more than fifty head of breeding stock, and from what Chet and Cody are telling me, all of 'em are bred and should be dropping calves in the spring. That's good that the bull did his job, but unfortunately your pa didn't realize how much those cows would be eatin' this winter. You just don't have enough land for pasturin' and still have enough extra grass to make hay for the winter. We've moved some of them down to our place, but we're going to have to start sellin' at least some of them off or we'll run out of the hay we've raised for our horses because the cows have been eatin' it too. I want you to be part of this and Cohen Lee wants to help us as well…"

Just then Lize scurried into the kitchen and started to stoke the fire in the stove and added more kindling wood. "Mr. Byron, Miz Callie, you two get yourselves outta my kitchen. I got bread to make and I'm goin' need this whole kitchen table for work.

Somewhat like a young child, Byron Harbison replied "Yes Ma'am" in a somewhat sarcastic tone, grabbed his cane and ushered Callie out to the porch to continue their conversation.

"Mr. Harbison, how did Lize get here? Was she born here? Did she live in the cabin with her mother and father before the war?" she asked pointing to the remains of the old slave cabin across the creek.

"No, my Pappy would never have let her live there, in fact, he couldn't because of a legal contract. She's always had that bedroom upstairs off the landing, at least as far as I can remember. You see she came here a few years before I was born. From what my pappy and ma told me it was kinda' a strange situation.

"Efron and Ellen Wilson were a young couple who lived down the road a piece from here when Pappy and Ma were young themselves. The Wilsons had a nice place with about two hundred acres that kept them workin' like the rest of the farmers from sun up to sundown, but they didn't have any family to help them. Ellen had a baby boy about a year after they got married and Efron had this idea. He told Ellen he had to go to St. Louis for a couple of days to get major supplies, but he'd be back with a special surprise for her and Efron Jr. on his return. The surprise was Lize.

He'd gotten a flyer about a boat full of slaves being brought up to St. Louis from the South, maybe New Orleans but I'm not sure, and that there were young girls for sale who were trained to be maids, housekeepers, cooks and mammies—that they could be bought in advance with a $100 deposit and another $500 when they picked 'em up. It was just like buyin' a wagon or a plow that you didn't want somebody else to buy before you got there. And you couldn't change your mind because a contract was signed.

"But it was kinda' like buyin' a pig in a poke," Pops chuckled. "When Efron got thar with his paperwork, the riverboat captain presented him with this little colored girl that couldn't a been more than eight or nine years old. When Efron said that wasn't what he had ordered, the captain said the child would be sent back down river and made a field hand somewheres. The little gal was already cryin', saying she wanted her ma. It was a sad sight. Efron took the little gal home and Ellen worn't too happy, but said she'd give the little gal a try.

"They fixed up a little place for her to sleep in a back room and over a week's period, taught her how to change diapers and take care of little Efron. The following week they had work to do in the field and told Lize to take care of the baby and they'd be back at noon."

Callie watched the expressions on Pops' face change as he continued his story. The Wilsons returned later to find Lize

77

wading in the pond up to her waist as she held tight to a metal washtub with little Efron inside.

"I'ze givin' him a boat ride like I got," she told the young couple.

Ellen Wilson screamed as she ran to rescue her six-month old son. After the baby was inside and safe she told her husband that that little darkie was no longer welcome.

"Now keep in mind I wasn't born yet, but I found papers in Pappy's desk that explained the situation," Pops said. Efron gave Lize to Pappy but there was legal papers that he had to sign first. Pappy agreed that Lize would be raised inside this house, that she was to be cared for properly with food and clothing, and that she'd get a hundred dollars a year for herself.

"Pappy had two slaves before the war who lived across the creek, but Lize always lived here and helped my ma raise me and my two brothers—but she kept an eye on her for a long time before she ever left her alone with us—especially if the creek was up," he said with a chuckle.

"What about the other slaves?" Callie asked. "Were they freed after the war?"

"Yes and no," Pops answered. "We had two of 'em that lived in that cabin and they were treated pretty darn well to my way of thinkin.' One, Caleb, was a younger man and a hard worker. The other, Everett, was one of the laziest and stealingest men I'd ever heard about. Pappy and Ma fed them what we ate and they even let them go to town on their own.

Everett would tie one on from stolen corn squeazins' almost every time he left the place.

"Around the war's end about a dozen blue coats, who were more likely deserters, raided the place and stole about a dozen mules from Pappy. They made off with everything in the smokehouse as well. They pulled their guns on Caleb and Everett, told them they were free and then ordered them to tie them mules together and follow them to the "freedom land" all while pointing their pistols at them.

"Caleb came back about a month after we heard the war was really over—came to give the mule back that he left on and said he was gettin' forty acres and another mule from the government up near Robertsville. Pappy shook his hand and told him to keep the mule—that those government mules weren't worth a damn compared to a Harbison mule. Heard he married a colored woman up there and they had a bunch of young'uns."

"Things didn't turn out as well for Everett," Pappy said. "He stayed with them marauders. Word spread about them, and when they rode into some little place south of here the town folks shot 'em to pieces. Everett was only wounded, and that wasn't enough for them folks. They stripped him down and hanged him on Main Street. There was even a photographer there who took pictures of the lynching. He made post cards out of the pictures and sold them for thirty-five cents. A cousin even mailed one to Pappy as a souvenir. Pappy caught me lookin' at it after I found it in his desk drawer years later. I got a lickin' for snoopin' and he tore it up and throwed it away."

Just then Beth came out to the porch with little Cody in her arms.

"Poppa Harbison, your wife has given me permission to take you up to the general store and get you a new shirt for the big dance comin' up," she said with a big smile on her face. She and Lize are gonna take care of Cody so I can help pick out one that doesn't look like all the others you have!"

Byron raised his eyebrows and agreed. Beth handed Cody off to Lize in the kitchen and proceeded to take her father-in-law by the arm and lead him down to the buggy that had already been hitched.

"Okay, I'm a goin' but there's nothin' wrong with the shirts I've got." His protesting got him nowhere and soon Ma's bucksin gelding was clip clopping towards town while Beth continued to talk about everything and anything to her father-in-law. As usual, Byron nodded in agreement but likely didn't listen to a word she had said.

Meanwhile, Callie found herself in the kitchen with Helen Harbison trying to rock a colicky Cody Jr. to sleep while Lize began to roll out kneaded dough on the kitchen table. The baby continued to be restless and soon howled at the top of his lungs. Helen was at wits' end.

Callie looked at Helen, and much to her surprise, heard her order to the black woman. "Give this child a teat to quiet him down or we'll never get this bread baked," Helen said.

Lize showed a grimace of displeasure, took the baby from Helen Harbison's arms and unbuttoned the top half of her blouse, exposing her left breast to the baby. She obeyed the order but didn't like it one bit. She placed the baby's mouth to her chest knowing that the child was cutting teeth and suckling her nipple would include the pain of a sharp tooth breaking through his gums.

I thought there wouldn't be no more of this of babies suckin' and pinchin' on me, she said to herself as she rocked the husky baby in her arms.

Lize had good life compared to many of the former slaves in the area but there were two things that she didn't like, but never refused to do. One was acting as a human pacifier for babies that included brothers Cody and Chet when they were younger, and other babies when families were visiting the farm. She had never had children of her own, or a man of her own, but she was expected to do the chore when asked.

The other tradition that she abhorred was Saturday bath night. It was her job to spread the towels and fill the large metal tub with hot water. The men of the house would bathe first and then she would empty the tub, bucket by bucket, wipe it out and refill with water from the stove. Then the women were allowed in the house with more hot water being added by Lize when needed. After the women and the children finished it was her turn.

"I might as well bathe in a muddy pond," she said to herself one hot summer evening as she scrubbed herself with a brush. But then she tried to think of the funny things in her life. She laughed thinking to herself about the mess Cody and Chet had made taking a bath one time when they were youngsters. The two boys were playing soldiers and had found the trap door in the hallway that led to the tunneled-out

crawl space that their grandfather had dug out as a possible escape route from bushwhackers during the War Between the States. When Helen found them, both were covered in dirt from head to toe. Lize was ordered to scrub them down good in the tub, as a lesson not to go under the house again.

They complained the entire time I was cleaning those boys up, she thought to herself. *They must have left an inch of mud in the bottom of that bathtub and had splashed muddy water all over the kitchen floor.*

Lize had one colored friend in town, Hannah, who lived on a family farm much in the same way that Lize did. They would sit together in the back row during church services and spend time together at church picnics. Hannah, at various times, had tempted Lize to pack up her small amount of belongings and go with her to St. Louis where they could truly be free and find their fortune. Lize had considered the idea at first. That was until she was invited to go to the big city for a day of shopping with Mr. and Mrs. Harbison. Fortunately the couple had made arrangements to stay with Pops' friend Mr. Langer. As they drove down the cobblestone streets she continued to see building after building that said, "whites only." In most of the shop visits Lize was allowed in with Mrs. Harbison but on at least two occasions she was told to stay in the buggy "because it would be better that way."

In Grubville, Lize was welcome in the general store and often did shopping on her own, especially at the end of the month when she had $8.04 to buy things for herself. On one such day she was admiring a bolt of fabric when an out-of-towner looked over and saw her.

"If you want me to buy something here, you had better get that nigger out of here right now," the man demanded. Mr. Nelson stammered not knowing exactly what to say. The man and his wife had already placed a large number of items on the counter.

Just then Cody and his father entered and Mr. Nelson heard Byron clear his throat.

"That woman can shop here," Nelson said with some hesitation.

"If you don't throw the nigger out, I will," the man demanded.

Byron cleared his throat one more time and then grabbed his cane by its bottom and pushed the crook of it against the man's chest forcing him against the wall where the harnesses were hanging.

Cody had never seen his father this angry—and neither had Lize. Although Byron needed the help of a cane to walk, his arms were as strong as they had ever been.

"That girl works for me," he said to the man as Byron pointed to Lize who was at least eight years his senior. "If you want her out, you'd better put me out first!"

Cody had a hard time not cracking a smile. Poor Lize, as pleased as she was with Mr. Harbison's gallantry, was afraid the bigger stranger was about to throw a punch. Perhaps Cody's large frame standing behind his father made the outsider rethink his intentions, or perhaps it was Byron's dominant tone of voice. Regardless, as Byron released the pressure of his cane, the man walked over to the counter and sheepishly paid his bill. Cody held the door open for him as the man and his wife departed.

Lize gave a sigh of relief and sat down in the wooden chair next to the stove and wiped her brow. She looked up at Byron. "Thank you so much. He sure was a mean man with a temper," she said.

"Ain't nobody goin' mess with my family," Byron said. Without missing a beat, he sauntered over to the counter," Nelson, did you ever get that pipe tobacco in I asked for?"

THE BARN DANCE

The long-awaited barn dance arrived and all the Harbison women, including Callie and Lize, were decked out in new homespun dresses. The men, although they preferred not to, were in their Sunday-go-to-meeting clothes. In reality they looked forward to the event as well. Pete McKinney had, as always, volunteered to be the caller at the square dance, and he among others, had a little something to add to the punch from flasks in their pockets, once the dipper was in use to pour refreshments into their cups.

On Callie's insistence Pops used Mr. Cavanaugh's Studebaker surrey with the fringed canopy top but he insisted on using his matched set of bay geldings to pull it. The larger buggy allowed for Callie to be joined by Beth and Little Cody, along with Mr. and Mrs. Harbison, and Lize. With Beth holding Little Cody, the other women braced for the drive holding various types of cakes and pies. One never knew if Pops might want to show off his team if someone tried to pass him on the way to the hoedown.

Although Chet decided to leave his Brook's Brothers suit in the closet, he did wear his best shirt and pants from before the war, along with a new broad-brimmed white Stetson he had ordered a month earlier. He on top of Red and Cody straddling a sturdy five-year-old chestnut led the way to the dance with the handsome carriage following.

Clapping, screeching fiddles, a twanging banjo, the strumming of a guitar and even the scuffing of a tin washboard could be heard as the family approached the large auction barn where the Harbisons sold horses and mules. As they entered, the ever-smiling George Timmons greeted the family. Saying hello to each of the Harbison men was easy for the man but his speech stumbled as he tried to say hello to Beth and Callie. Beth eased the awkwardness of the family friend by giving him a hug and a peck on his cheek. It followed by Cody grabbing the man's shoulder and telling him to keep his hands off of "his woman." Poor George took a minute to understand the action as a joke, but then slapped his friend's back saying, "You know I wouldn't do anything like that."

Lize scampered to one of the corners of the barn to greet her friend Hannah after helping Mrs. Harbison and Callie take the pies and cakes to the tables along the back wall.

The music continued and men and women, changed partners to the screeching calls of Pete McKinney. Lori Simpson, with her flaxen hair in curls, wearing a long free-flowing red satin skirt and a store-bought low-cut white silk blouse, showed off her well-endowed chest as she talked to the single men in the barn. The ruffles along her collar made her breasts catch the attention of those gathered on the sawdust floor. Men and women, young and old, took notice, including Beth, Callie—and Chet. After what seemed to be an eternity, the music slowed down for a waltz. Byron took his wife's hand and entered the center of the barn to dance, as did some of the other mature folks.

Meanwhile, Pete headed for the refreshments while reaching for a flask in his coat pocket to add some more "flavor" to his drink. By now, Lize was bouncing Little Cody on her knee while Beth encouraged Big Cody to join her on the dance floor. He accepted, although with reluctance, leaving Callie, Chet and his buddy Pete sitting on chairs and sipping punch provided by Pete—much to Callie's surprise it had a unique taste compared to any other punch she had ever consumed.

It was awkward for the two as the slow music continued with Callie wondering if she would be asked to dance and Chet wanting to ask but being afraid she might think him to be too "forward."

Thoughts of all three changed when they spied Lori almost prancing—and bouncing—in their direction. Callie's face turned a reddish tint, the same as it did when she was embarrassed, but this time it was from anger. Chet's face did the same with perspiration starting to form on his forehead. He'd rather be facing a wild bronc than the woman who had ripped his heart out more than a year ago.

Pete sprang to his feet and almost tripped over himself getting to the Simpson girl. Being as short as he was, while reaching for her waist for a slow dance, his right hand ended up clutching the upper half of her buttocks while he grabbed her right hand with his left. She yanked at his wrist moving his hand another five inches higher.

"Gal, I've been wanting to dance with you ever since I saw you over at Wheeler's the other week," he said. With that he leaned the right side of his face upon the uncovered part of her breast and began to dance. Lori was so caught off guard that she went along with it, but shook the boys head with her chest and ordered him to look at her when they danced.

It's now or never, Chet thought. With that, he looked into Callie's eyes and asked, "It there the slightest chance that the prettiest girl in the county would take my hand to dance?"

"That girl, I believe, is dancing with Pete," she joked back. "But I sure would like to dance with a courageous Rough Rider," she said, escaping from her bashfulness.

Pete went back to calling when the music changed, and as he started his routine he did a double-take as he saw Lori latched onto none other than George Timmons with a grip as tight as a vice.

"Oh George, I've been waiting to see you all night," she said while dragging the poor man to the center of the dance floor, close to Chet and Callie. The country boy and city girl were at ease, dancing and talking, not paying attention anyone in the barn, including Lori Simpson.

George was overjoyed with the attention he was receiving, but was confused. This was the girl who had called him "simple" at a church gathering this past summer and the same girl who all but ignored him when he visited her father's lumber mill to have oak logs ripped into boards for fencing and barn raisings. Much to his astonishment she kissed him on his neck several times and even whispered into his ear that she loved down-to-earth "working men."

What he didn't notice is that most of the moves she was making took place when they danced near Chet and Callie.

And there was no way George could see her wink at Chet when his eyes strayed in her direction.

As the evening wore down and young babies and children began whining because it was past their bedtimes, families began gathering their belongings and heading toward home. The Harbisons were among them as young Cody showed the gathering that he had a set of lungs as loud as any of the babies who were brought to the dance by their mothers and fathers.

As Chet walked Cassie outdoors to the carriage, Lori Simpson made one more stab at Chet's heart.

"Oh George, I had such a great time with the most handsome man here," she said. "Could you take me home?"

George looked behind himself when he heard the words "handsome man" come from her mouth, thinking she was speaking of someone else.

"I got no buggy Miss Simpson, and I'm afeared that pretty outfit of yours would get all messed up and dirty if we was to ride double on Hotshot."

"No, no, no," she insisted as the Harbisons filed by. "I have a buggy. You can tie your horse onto the back and take me home. It's so dark going down the road to my daddy's place. I'm afraid to go by myself."

"I'd be afraid to go down that dark road with that woman if it were me," Cody Harbison whispered into Beth's ear as they walked by. "I think I'd rather tangle with a bobcat than have that gal git her hooks into me."

Beth reached up to her husband with her right hand, hitting the back of his head and knocking his wide-brimmed brown hat to the ground. "You keep gawking at that hussy and you're goin' think a bobcat is mild compared to what I'm goin' to do to you," she said with a mischievous look on her face.

"Yes ma'am," Cory said, saluting to his wife. He picked up his hat and began dusting it off as Beth smacked his behind as they walked toward the carriage. It didn't hurt but it got his attention.

When the family arrived back at the farm, Pebbles was there to greet them. As usual, he didn't bark, but jumped up on Helen, Beth, and Cassie, as if to welcome them back after a long night.

"Cody, you and Pops go on in," Chet said. "I'll put up the bays in their stalls and take care of Red and Sonny Boy as well."

There was no arguing on Cody's part. Besides, whenever Chet wanted to spend extra time with the horses it usually meant he had some heavy thoughts on his mind to hash through. This must have been one of those times. Besides, Cody had noticed that Beth was still bragging to her mother-in-law about the wonderful time she had and wished they could hold more dances. And who knows, maybe she was feeling a little frisky tonight. Maybe Lize could even keep Cody in her room for part of the night.

A half an hour later, Chet sauntered up to the porch where he found Cassie sitting on the squeaky porch swing.

"My, oh my, this is a pleasant surprise," he said as he placed himself onto the center section of the three-person swing and placed his arm around Callie's shoulders. "I must have died and gone to heaven having a sweet little thing like you a waitin' for me."

"Chester Harbison! Did you drink too much of Pete's punch? I haven't seen you so outspoken and happy since you got home from Cuba."

"Maybe I did drink a little of it, but in all seriousness, I'm in such a good mood because all my troubles and worries went away tonight when I was with you."

"You shouldn't have any troubles now," she said. "You're at home with those who love you very, very much. Is it those Spragg boys who have got you worrying?"

"It's not them at all Cassie," Chet said. He hesitated, but then decided to continue. "I've been on edge more than not since I got back and I'm not sure why. I think it must be because of Cuba. Me and Ritchie and the other men were always lookin' for them Spaniards because you'd never knew if they were watchin' you are not. I know they're not here, but I'm still lookin' over my shoulder for them or somebody. But I'm not lookin' as much as when I got here, and I didn't look for them at all tonight—not with you bein' with me."

With that, Chet stared into Callie's eyes and kissed her. She closed her eyes and realized it was the first time she had ever been kissed by a boy.

"Miss Callie, you get yourself in here right now! Chester, you get up to your room!"

The couple jumped when they heard the demanding order from Lize.

"We better do what she says or she'll be throwin' a cold bucket of water on both of us," Chet said.

Helen Harbison stood at the counter with Lize putting away the leftovers from the dance. "I'm so glad you two had such a good time," she said. Then Helen and Lize watched as Callie entered her room and Chet climbed the stairs to his small bedroom up above. The two women looked at each other in approval and went to their own rooms. Pops, who was in the dining room, inhaled one last time on his pipe and grinned. He knocked the ashes into an empty peach can that sat on the table and followed his wife to bed, closing the door behind him.

GEORGE—THE WISE MAN

Cody Harbison was back in his work clothes after church Sunday morning. The circuit preacher didn't show and Wheeler Frost, a man of few words, was asked to read from the Bible—a suggestion made by Byron Harbison and seconded by Cohen Lee. Both were tired from staying up late at the dance and they knew from experience that Wheeler would make his point in twenty minutes or less, much to the displeasure of the folks that Pops often referred to as "the high and the mighty."

With a pitchfork in hand, Cody was tossing hay from the top of the stallion barn into the large staked wagon below. If pastureland was to be saved for next spring, the Cavanaugh cattle and Harbison brood mares and young foals alike had to be started on winter hay before the cold weather set in with freezing temperatures and snow.

Wiping the sweat from his brow, Cody noticed George Timmons coming down the road on his prized possession, a sorrel-colored blanket appaloosa gelding.

It's Sunday. What the hell is George doing here on his day off? Maybe he had a little too much punch and forgot what day it was.

As the horse got closer to the barn Cody could see that George was still wearing his good shirt from the night before, but the man's curly hair was disheveled and he had a full day's growth of whiskers on his face. It was then that Cody remembered that George had left the dance with no one other than the notorious Lori Simpson. Cody climbed down the ladder from the loft and greeted George as he tied his horse to the paddock railing.

George walked up to his friend but continued to look down at the ground. "Cody, you're my best friend," George said. "I need to talk to ya'. Do you promise this won't go any further than me and you?"

"You bet partner," Cody said. "What's this all about?"

"Well, it's kinda' embarrassin' but I need to talk it through with someone. That Simpson gal was all over me like stink on a skunk last night, tellin' me how much she always liked me, when she'd never even gived me the time of day ever. Then she asked me to drive her home in her buggy even though she knows I live in the cottage behind Wheeler's and there was no need for me to go way down Morse Mill Road to that big house her daddy got after his father-in-law spit the bit."

By now, Cody was holding his chin with this hand, wanting to know more, but too afraid to ask.

"We go about a quarter mile from thar when she had me stop the buggy. And if you think she was a huggin' and a pullin' on me at the dance, it weren't nothing compared to on that dark, dirt road."

If Cody had been jaw bonin' with Chet, Pete or any of the other boys from town, he would have been grinning ear to ear, but he'd never seen George so serious and maybe even scared in his whole life.

"It got really wild," George said. "She started a teasin' me, movin' all around, getting' me all nervous—kinda' like that fancy palomino mare that fella brought down here from the city to have ol' Monty breed with her. Remember how she danced around and frustrated that horse almost to death before she finally gave in to him?"

"Yeah, I sure do," Cody said. By now the older Harbison brother was holding his hand over his mouth with his red bandana, faking like he was wiping the sweat off of his face.

"For a little-boned gal like she is, she sure has large udders and she bared 'em to me and was a pushin' 'em in my face like I was a nursin' calf."

Cody couldn't hold back any more. He leaned back against the paddock gate and started laughing so hard he dropped to his knees. Poor George looked serious, maybe even mad, and then thought for a second and started laughing almost as hard as Cody.

"Well ya' know, it was kinda' fun and excitin'," George grinned. "Yup it was fun and excitin'. I guess I was a feelin' like ol' Monty last night, wasn't I?"

"Yep, I bet you was," Cody said as they both started to calm down. "But George, two things: If it ever comes up, I think you should refer to a girl's 'udders' as her 'chest' instead. That way she won't think you're comparing her to Guernsey cow. And I gotta ask, did ya', uh, uh, 'mount' her?"

George looked down at the dirt and blushed. "Uh, not exactly. That girl is all touchy, feely like and her hands started a wanderin' and I uh, I uh…"

"No, no! That's enough George. You don't have to go into details. I understand." Cody said.

Then George got serious again.

"When I put away her horse and walked her to those big old doors of her house, she done gave me another big kiss and said to keep it all a big secret—but that I could tell my friend Chet. I thought about it all the way back to my place, and all night. It finally hit me—she weren't interested in me a'tall. She did it thinkin' that if Chet found out about it he would be mad at me, or want to get back with her or somethin' like that. Ya' know, she called me 'simple' up at the picnic this summer and then last night, well, you know. I knowed that there ain't no girls interested in dumb ol' George—especially Lori Simpson."

"George, if I ever thought you were, as you say, 'simple,' I know I would be a damn fool for ever believin' it. You're one of the wisest men in these here parts, I do believe—especially when it comes to figurin' out women folk. You mighta' had some fun with her sparkin' you the way she did but you're way too good a human bein' for that little tramp. Just because her daddy has money, doesn't make her better than you and me."

Cody paused for a moment.

James R. Wilder

"George, I know you think you may never find a girl of your own, but I think you're wrong. There's a little gal out there somewhere," Cody said as he raised his arm and pointed his finger, swinging his arm in a semi circle toward the rolling hills of the farm. "You're goin' find yourself a girl as pretty and smart as my Beth some day. Just you wait and see. And another thing you're smart about: Let's not tell what happened to you to anybody. It will be our little secret."

With that George spit a gob on the palm of his right hand and reached out to "shake on it" with Cody. Cody, with slight hesitation, extended his hand and shook. George turned to the house as Helen Harbison walked out to the porch and raised her voice.

"George, will you have dinner with us? It's nearly noon and it's almost ready," she said. "We've even got some peach cobbler left over from last night."

"Yes'm Mrs. Harbison," George said. "I'd be right pleased to join you all."

Cody wiped his hand on the side of his jeans, put his arm around George's shoulder and walked back to the house. It hit him that George was truly his best friend as well.

97

DOWN TO BUSINESS

At Pops' suggestion, Callie began to make handbills to advertise the sale of fifteen of her father's registered black Aberdeen Angus cows. Mr. Lee offered to distribute the bills along his mail route and encouraged Callie to come along so she could learn the skills of being a "true salesman." Pops and Mr. Lee had agreed that selling the cows outright would bring a better price than taking a chance at the auction as the cold weather set in. They also took out an ad in the county newspaper. Callie prepared the write-up for the printer. She had been forced to listen to all the bragging her father had done about the Aberdeen Angus, and now it was paying off because she knew more about their lineage than that of a typical farmer in the area.

And Cohen Lee wasn't really bragging when he took credit for being a "true salesman." While honest in nature it was said the man could have sold hot coals to the devil himself in the month of August.

Although he jumped at taking the job as a rural route deliveryman to ease into a less-hectic life, Cohen had always been a salesman. He'd travel throughout the country—even as far as New York. His specialty included watches, clocks, and thermometers, but after returning home he would buy and sell just about anything he came upon. That included livestock, wagons, the now-popular sewing machines, and farm implements. He always made money, but he always charged a fair price. If a farmer in the region needed to buy an expensive piece of equipment, he'd always contact Cohen before going to the city or checking the Sears and Roebuck or Montgomery Ward catalogs.

Callie got her first taste of Mr. Lee's personality after arranging to meet him early one Monday morning at his farm at the start of his mail delivery.

She was becoming more and more fond of Helen's Buck, but there were times when she wished the old gelding would pick up his heels a little faster. By now Callie was saddling the horse on her own and if she had any trouble at all Chet, Cody, Beth—and even George Timmons—were there to help.

Pebbles, the spotted part-collie that had been rescued by Helen Harbison had taken it upon himself to go along—at least as far as Mr. Lee's place—and then would return home after some of his own investigating of the area.

"That thar dog of Helen's is a smart and guardful dog, young lady," Mr. Lee said as Callie rode up to the corral where the mail wagon was hitched.

"I had a 'coon dog by the name of Sam that was a might smarter though."

"How's that?" Callie asked.

Mr. Lee had reeled her in hook, line, and sinker. It was the question he wanted her to ask.

"Well, he was smart in a lot of ways," Mr. Lee said with a twinkle in his eyes. "Some ways he was smarter than others.

Now, you take playin' checkers. He wasn't that good. I could always beat him—at least two out of three times, that is."

Callie knew she was in for more. She watched as the man stood there with a smile on his face as he began to tell his yarn.

He's a real storyteller, she thought to herself. *And his looks, well they're different for sure. He doesn't have a hair on his head but his eyebrows are as thick as can be. And he's shorter than me. And for a man a little older than Mr. Harbison he sure has broad shoulders. But what's unique is his craggily sounding voice.*

"But darned if that dog could hunt 'coon better'n any other hound dog I ever knowed," Mr. Lee said. "Fact of the matter is, I could come out of the barn with a foot-and-a-half-long piece of lumber and show it to that dog and he'd take off a howlin' and a runnin' as fast as he could. Within an hour or so he'd come back draggin' a raccoon from his mouth. After I'd wrestled it away from him I could set that 'coon alongside that board and it would be within an inch of its length.

"I lost 'im though," he said. "It was a heapin' shame."

"Well what happened to him?" Callie asked. This time her eyes were rolling. She'd figured him out.

"Well, my missus, Marcella, had to pack up some things to visit her ailin' aunt over in Catawissa. With her aunt bedridden there hadn't been a lot of washin' and ironin' goin' on, so she ordered me to take that ironin' board of hers and put it in the back of the mail wagon. When I came out of house with that long wooden board, old Sam cocked his head and gave a strange look that I ain't never seen before. Sure enough, he started a howlin' and ran off toward the woods. I ain't seen hide nor hair of him since. But I swear, I can still hear him at night sometimes howlin' away lookin' for that giant raccoon that don't exist."

"I think we should get on the road," Callie said, hardly being able to speak because of her giggling.

"Yes ma'am!" he said as he did a mock salute.

Sure enough, as she rode with Mr. Lee there were farmers and ranchers who were interested in the Cavanaugh breeding stock. But knowing the situation they wanted and expected to buy the cows at bargain pricing. Mr. Lee wouldn't let that happen. First, because he became very fond of Callie, second because he was one of Byron Harbison's best friends, and last because Pops and Callie had agreed Mr. Lee should receive a small percentage of every sale he helped make.

As the two travelled the dirt roads of Jefferson County the offers varied. Most of the low offers were followed by "I'd pay more but the Almanac says we've got a tough winter coming on. I can save a lot of hay and silage if I don't buy until spring."

"And by then, those cows will be with calves and you'll have to pay nearly twice as much for them," Cohen would tell the farmer. "And they won't be registered breeding stock like this young lady owns. You'll not only get a good breeding cow with us, you'll have a fifty-fifty chance to get one of the finest seed bulls from these here parts. If'en it's a heifer, you come out of the bargain almost as good."

About half the time, the farmer, if he truly knew good stock, would come up in price, and almost every time, Cohen would allow for haggling and let the man take his pick of the cows and let him have it for a few dollars less than the original bargain.

"It makes a fellow feel like he really got a sweet deal without us losin' our shirts, so to speak," Cohen told Callie.

During one of the inquiries, the farmer Alvin Scroggins told Callie he would have to think about it and get back with her next week.

"Sir, I've got quite a few folks who told me that very same thing three or four days ago," she said. There's even a man from St. Clair who wants to buy ten of them. There's a good chance we might not have any cows left by next week and you'll have to lower your standards and buy from someone else."

"Cohen," Scroggins said. "I think this Cavanaugh gal has been spending too much time with you. I'll meet you two at the Harbison farm this afternoon at 2 o'clock to pick out three cows. If she goes out on her own, you're going to have to find another way to earn a livin'. I think she's a tad better at sellin' than you and a lot prettier to boot."

With that Cohen flipped the reins saying "gitty up, Dollie." He turned to Callie and smiled. "I can't take no commission on them three cows young lady. You did it all on your own."

Callie blushed and then turned back to him. "Gee, I guess I did. Not bad for a city girl, huh?" They both laughed and continued on the mail route.

Along those dusty roads while delivering mail and buying and selling, Callie questioned Mr. Lee about the history of the area, the folks who lived there—and about Chet Harbison.

"That boy is quite a character," Mr. Lee said. Between him and his brother, and that McKinney boy, they stirred up more dust than any of the other young'uns in these here parts. And if you think I'm good at spinnin' yarns and sellin', that Chet is among the best. He always was walkin' around with a grin on his face and a story to tell. He didn't smile nearly as much when he came back from that blasted war, but he seems to be smiling a lot more now that's he's gotten to know you a little better, young lady."

"Oh, tell me more," she said

"Well, there was the time that Pete bet that boy he didn't have the sand to ride his gelding into Nelson's store. There was a whole dollar ridin' on it, so to speak. Chet upped the ante to five dollars, tellin' Pete he could ride that critter up the back steps, down the stairs and out the front door. He was about twelve or thirteen at the time and had this gray gelding that would just about do anything for the boy.

"That horse came prancin' out the front of Nelson's with Chet wearin' a woman's sun bonnet on his head. Nelson was right behind him with a broom swattin' at him and that horse. That boy was laughin' so hard I thought he was goin' fall out of the saddle.

"When it was all over, the boy gave Nelson the five dollars he'd won in the bet and got a shovel, and then a scrub bucket and brush to clean up the mess after that gelding got a little excited while comin' down those steps. Then he had to face his pa when he got home—word spreads awful quick around here. If Byron hadn't been such a prankster when he was a boy, there's no tellin' what he would have done to him. Helen was even more embarrassed and didn't even want to go up to Nelson's store since the ordeal reflected on her parenting.

"But even Nelson didn't take it too bad," Cohen said. "When a twister came tearin' through town about six months earlier, it was those youngsters—Chet, Cody, and Pete—who were the first ones there a checkin' on him and his family and then spent two days a pickin' up and pilin' up all the scrap lumber and tin roofin'. They also helped pick up all the sundries and supplies that were tossed about for more than a mile. The rest of us folks all pitched in too, if'en we weren't busy with our own storm damage.

"Then there was the time that McKinney boy hitched up his pa's high-steppin' saddle horse to a buggy I had on the side of my place. Word got out that it was Chet who gave him the idea. That poor horse had never seen a harness its life. When Pete got in the seat and shook the reins that ol' horse took out like a bat out of hell—I mean Hades—and broke just about every spoke on every wheel before he got it stopped. That was the summer that Pete worked for me without pay when he wasn't workin' for his pa. Chet came around and helped him a lot in his spare time, knowin' he was part to blame. They'd work hard and I'd treat 'em to a sarsaparilla from time to time.

By Thanksgiving the herd was down from fifty to thirty head, counting the bull.

"Callie, I believe you now have enough hay and silage to get those cows through the winter," Pops told her as he sliced the goose that Helen and Lize had prepared for the holiday meal. And if not, we've got a little extra. You'll still have a good crop of calves to sell this spring."

"I don't know how to thank all of you for taking me in," she said. "You make me feel like family." With Chet sitting next to her, she felt his hand touch hers underneath the dining room table. She was beginning to feel like family to everyone at the table but her feelings for Chet were different.

THE HUNT

The moonlight stole through a crack in the curtains of Byron and Helen Harbison's bedroom and with it Byron rolled closer to the edge of the bed, reached in the direction of his alarm clock and pushed the peg to silence the clatter of the clappers before they even started. It was 5 o'clock on a cold and crisp December morning. Frost was on the window and a light dusting of snow had fallen overnight. He reached for his bib overalls and shirt that were tossed over the back of a nearby chair and then for his cane that was leaning against the small table near the bed.

As quiet as he was, Helen began to stir. "Why don't you wake one of the boys and take 'em with you Byron? They enjoy a good deer hunt as much as anyone."

"Naw, they need their sleep. They spent all day yesterday workin' the stock," he whispered. "Besides I plan on gettin' the biggest buck there is this year and I don't need no help from them youngsters."

"You're as stubborn as one of your mules," she said. "Just because you've got a bad hip doesn't mean you have to prove yourself every time the deer start a moving about."

"I'm not tryin' to prove any such thing to anybody," he protested. "I've been a seein' deer tracks all this fall when I went giggin' frogs along the stream just off Jones Creek

Road. And they were pretty big tracks. When I get him, we'll have plenty of venison to last us through the winter.

"You're not fooling me one iota," she said. "I saw that poster at Nelson's store just like you—twenty dollars and a picture in the county paper to whoever comes in with the biggest deer—and the contest is over at the end of the day. You told me yourself that Wheeler has got it all sewed up with that ten-point buck he shot Thursday."

"From the size of the tracks there's one out there that's three hundred and fifty pounds or better, and it'll put that little thing of Wheeler's to shame," Byron chuckled.

"You two are just like little children," she said. "If you fall out there don't expect me to go a looking for you. I'll just wait for the buzzards to start circling and send the boys out to get what's left of you," she said with a grin.

"Go back to sleep woman. I got to get ready and on my way."

"Be careful," she said.

He kissed his wife of almost thirty years on the cheek and shuffled to the kitchen where his rifle, cartridges, coat and hat were waiting. He stoked the stove and started to grind some coffee when he heard the kitchen door open. In walked Chet.

"Pops, I hitched one of your bays to the huntin' wagon and you're already to go."

"Your ma put you up to this didn't she? I've been hitching my own horses since I was seven and don't need no help. But thanks—an' no, you ain't comin' with me. That damn stray dog of your ma's will start a followin' me anyways as soon as he sees me with my rifle."

"Okay, okay," Chet said.

Byron poured a cup of coffee and sipped on it while he stashed two biscuits and a strip of jerky onto a kitchen towel, folded it and stuck it in his coat pocket. He placed a box of cartridges in the other pocket. Then he grabbed his red-and-black-checked hunting cap and untied the strings on the top of it. He took the brim between this thumb and index figure and pulled it down onto his head, flipped the earflaps down and then tied the strings under his chin. Taking his cane in one hand and his rifle in the other, he limped down the porch steps and along the stone covered path to the end of the walk where his horse and wagon waited. The wagon was special, and he called it his hunting wagon because when he built it he made it shorter and the axles narrower so it could travel down dirt paths on hunting trips. Byron had slipped on the ice that formed on the creek between the house and the stud barn one cold and dreary day and had broken his hip. He was a quick healer for a man of his age but he was left burdened with a distinctive limp and a loss of balance that forced him to use the cane. He never complained and everyone in the house, with the exception of Helen, never spoke of it. When he attempted to perform a duty that was an unlikely task for him, they let him do it. Most of the time he succeeded; however, everyone learned he wanted no applause for what he considered an everyday task.

The ride to Jones Creek was more of a challenge than the actual hunt. In daylight Pops drove his bay through the upper side of the north forty of the farm. It was rolling hills for the most part but the last mile would take the wagon through a narrow, rocky path before reaching Jones Creek Road. Besides, Pops didn't know for sure where his prize buck would stop for water along the stream, and that stream ran alongside of Jones Creek Road, more or less, for more than five miles. Instead, he directed the bay gelding to head for the main road towards town, but instead of heading north at the end of the farm road, he reined the horse south and headed for Morse Mill Road. It was a roundabout way, but he figured that if he reached the crossroads of Jones Creek Road by dawn he'd literally have a shot at one of the biggest bucks in Jefferson County. The deer population had dwindled in recent years because of overhunting by farmers who were facing hard times in feeding their families. As a result, it was difficult to find a buck of any substantial size.

As expected, the spotted dog was following behind.

Well at least that cur dog ain't likely to bark, Byron thought. Desperados could rustle every head of stock I have and that mutt wouldn't even growl.

As planned, the sun began to rise just as Byron approached his turnoff. If he had stayed on Morse Mill just a little longer he would have passed the Simpson House, a mansion by Grubville standards. It was whitewashed with four pillars across the front porch that reached up to the second story, but the most valuable item on the place was a large housed sawmill that used the rapid current of the Big River for power.

Orville Simpson married right, Byron thought. Ol' man Morse was on his last legs when Simpson proposed to his only daughter, who was a pretty little thing, but quite opinionated, boy howdy. And that daughter of theirs is cut from the same cloth. I don't know how that man puts up with either of 'em.

Anyone who needed wooden timbers, planks or cedar shakes came to Orville's place to have it cut. It was the only place within thirty miles and Orville was proud of his work when it came to price. He was a worker, though. He was the first one at the mill every morning and the last to leave. He knew it was his lifeblood. On the other hand, he never took it upon himself to run a log through the saw blade. There were hired hands for that—and many of those hands had fingers missing.

"Road" was a poor term. *Shoulda' called this Jones Creek Path*, Byron said to himself as he reined in as the ruts and rocks jolted the small wagon about. It took him another thirty minutes to get halfway down the path when he spied the buck he'd been looking for. He eased the bay to a stop and Pebbles ears perked up when she heard her somewhat of a master say, "Shh."

Byron moved at a fast pace for a man with a bad hip as he stepped down from the wagon and reached for his Winchester. High upon a rocky ledge overlooking the creek was what looked like a 16-point buck. From the angle down below, the beast looked as if it was more the size of an elk.

Darned if it don't look like the one on the calendar at Glen's barber shop in St. Louis, Byron thought. The beast was statuesque, standing straight and tall as it looked over the countryside from its high mountain perch. The morning sun rising behind the animal gave Byron a silhouette view.

Without making any unnecessary noise he cocked the lever-action rifle, put a bead on the deer and squeezed the trigger. The massive buck tumbled over the ledge, falling about fifteen feet to the ground, lodging itself in a gap between two rock formations near the edge of the creek.

Byron placed his rifle in the bed of the wagon and petted the bay's muzzle to calm him after it pranced about after hearing the report of the rifle. Once the gelding settled down, Byron, using his cane for balance, crossed the ice-covered flat stones to the other side of the creek.

"Damn it to hell," he said as he tugged on the deer's rack in an attempt to pull the slain animal from between the rocks. As strong as his upper torso was, Byron couldn't budge the animal more than an inch or two.

Pebbles and the horse both turned their attention to the hunter, appearing somewhat startled by the man's temper— Byron Harbison was not one to raise his voice without reason.

"Well boys, it looks like this old man is going to have to get some help if'en he's going to win that twenty bucks off of Nelson," he said turning to the dog and the horse. "This damn thing is so big I couldn't get it on the back of the wagon even if it weren't stuck between the rocks."

If I time it just right, I can turn this crate around and hightail it back to the gate that leads to the north forty. Cody and Chet can help me get this critter loose from the rocks and we'll take it up to Nelson's—and show it off to Wheeler and anyone else who are up in town.

"Come on Prince, let's see if you can make some time once we get off this God forsaken trail. The sure-footed bay took its time heading along the rocky road and then to the cutoff, an even narrower path that led to the back gate of the Harbison farm. Once they reached the rolling-hills section of the farm, Prince's hooves clipped along at a rapid pace. By now the sun was out and what snow had fallen the night before had turned to slush. Mud began to cake the wheels of the wagon but the horse continued at a fast pace.

When Byron arrived at the farmhouse, Helen was in the yard throwing feed to the chickens.

"Where's the boys? I got that buck but he's so damn big I couldn't fetch him by myself."

"Bite your tongue Byron, little Callie don't need to be hearing such talk," she said.

"If she didn't hear it from her father, she's surely heard it from Cohen," Byron snapped back.

By now Callie, Beth and Lize all came to the door to see what the commotion was about.

"Well she don't need it to hear it from you," Helen said. "Cody and Chet left about fifteen minutes ago after Wheeler sent George down to tell us a load of oats finally arrived for the horses. That horse of yours is started to lather up a bit. You'd better not push him so hard."

"He's fine—and stout enough to take on anyone ridin' a buggy that I'd see going into town."

Byron snapped the reins and Prince took off like he was in a race. Helen shook her head and went back to feeding the chickens that had been startled by the popping of the reins and surge of the bay horse.

"You girls quit your lollygagging and check the henhouse for eggs. Lize, we've got rugs to beat. Get them out here."

All three women acknowledged their orders, but all cracked smiles knowing she was fuming at her childlike husband and not them. With the hunt over, Pebbles found a sunny spot on the porch and took a morning nap.

The morning snow had already melted. The wagon-wheels' spokes continued to throw a spray of mud as the horse neared town. Sure enough, Byron spotted the hay wagon next to Wheeler's barn—half filled with burlap bags of oats. He slowed Prince down to a walk and a moment or two later reined in the lathered bay to the hitching rail. First, he provided the animal with a small drink of water from a bucket and then tied him to the post. For a man with a gimp leg, Byron Harbison was ambling at a quick walk when he swung open the screen door and then pushed open the solid oak door to Wheeler's store.

Both boys, along with Pete McKinney, were sitting on worn wooden kitchen chairs around the stove as Wheeler filled three coffee cups.

"Wheeler, pour me a cup of that varnish you call coffee," Byron said with a grin on his face. "Boys, those oats will have to wait a spell. And Wheeler, you can kiss that twenty bucks from Nelson goodbye because I just nailed the biggest deer I've ever see in in my life—must be pert' near four hundred pounds with the biggest rack I've ever seen."

"Well, we'll have to see about that," Wheeler said as he paused and viewed the ten or twelve antler racks mounted on the walls of his store.

"The damn thing is stuck between two boulders and I couldn't have lifted it anyways if it weren't," Byron said.

Byron sipped on his hot coffee waiting to hear some type of snide remark from his best friend the storeowner, but Wheeler had nothing more to say. Cody and Chet finished their coffee about the same time as their father and put on their coats. Pete acknowledged he'd join them in a minute. For once the brothers were having a hard time keeping up with their father who was as jumpy as a young pup. Wheeler decided to follow.

Pops stopped in his tracks as he exited the feed store. He spotted the gigantic buck atop the large scale that was situated on the loading dock of Nelson's general store. Wheeler and Nelson bought it together several years ago to weigh planting seed, livestock grain, and slaughtered beef and pork. Walking closer to the scale, Byron saw the needle pointing to the numbers indicating that the brute weighed in at 377 pounds.

Chet's eyes were not on the scale. He noticed the tall pinto mare with a Mexican saddle tied up along the hitching rail, and then turned to see two other riders on scruffy-looking horses heading north out of town.

"That son of a bitch Spragg has finally done it," Chet said. "He's not pulling this shit with us anymore!"

"Calm down, son," Pops said. "Believe it or not, I've got this under control. But I think you, Cody, and Wheeler, might want to watch."

Cody scratched his head in disbelief, rolled his eyes and followed the others into the general store where they found Nelson fiddling with his like-new Kodak Brownie box camera.

"Now Dutch, you might not get your picture in the paper for a while after I make it for you. The instructions here from Eastman Kodak says this thing will make a hundred pictures and I've only taken twenty-three since I bought it last spring," Nelson said.

"I don't need no picture, old man," Dutch Spragg said as he slammed his fist onto the countertop. I need my damn money so I can get out of this hell hole you call a town."

Nelson began counting out a couple of five-dollar bills and then some ones as Byron walked up to the cash register.

"Better hold onto that money for a spell Nelson," Byron said. "That buck out front is mine. I shot it less than an hour ago down on Jones Creek. The boys were just going to retrieve it for me."

"You're lying old man!" Dutch said. "I shot that deer on the way up here from Big River right at daylight. And you can't prove otherwise. Now step aside, you worthless cripple."

George Timmons, who also was inside the store, stood in disbelief. Why would anyone say something to be so mean to a man as nice as Mr. Harbison?

Chet had had enough and was about to tear into the eldest of the Spragg boys, but Pops held out his arm. "Calm down Chet. I've got this under control."

"Trust your pa," Wheeler whispered while keeping a big grin on his face. "You ain't seen nothin' yet."

"Boy, I've been called a lot worse by a lot better than the likes of you and I'll bet that twenty dollars Nelson's got in his hands against the twenty in my back pocket that that buck is mine and you're nothin' but a ornery liar yourself. First of all, you don't even have a rifle with you or on that fancy horse of your'n."

"You can't prove nothin', old man! My brothers just left with my rifle for more hunting. I want my twenty bucks now!"

Nelson stepped back, away as far as he could, leaning against the canned goods on the shelf behind him to the point that a can of peaches got bumped and fell to the floor.

Byron walked up closer to the counter, reached into his coat pocket and slammed a deer's tongue onto the counter, splattering blood onto Dutch's sleeve. Alice Hoffman who was watching from behind the potato bin gasped, "Oh, how disgusting!"

"Chet, I told ya' your pa had him to rights," Wheeler said.

"Boy, on your way out—without that money, mind you— you'll find that buck is missing his tongue, and the knife cuts on this tongue will be a perfect match to what's missing from what's left in that critter's mouth. You have a good day now, boy."

Dutch's face turned red as everyone in the store began to laugh. Cody slapped his father on the shoulder for the move he had made before leaving the deer behind.

But Dutch wasn't through. He reached over the counter, yanking the paper bills from Nelson's hands. Then he plowed into Byron, knocking him off balance and causing the older Harbison's head to hit the corner of the counter before he stumbled to the wooden floor of the general store.

As Cody bent over to help his father up, Chet lunged for Dutch, who by now had reached the threshold of the door.

Pete McKinney was just walking up the steps to the store, chomping on an apple, when he jumped back, seeing Spragg and his best friend come sliding out the door on their bellies with Chet's arms wrapped around Dutch's calves.

"Looks like I got here just in time," Pete said as Cody and a disheveled Pops peered out the door.

Sliding off the dock and into the mud both men jumped to their feet with fists in the air.

"This is the last time I want to see you in this town you hunk of shit!" With that Chet took a swing, clipping Dutch's chin.

"Well, soldier boy, you don't seem too tough to me. Maybe you ought to go help your old man home to his rockin' chair."

The next left hook connected, hitting Dutch square in the jaw, but was returned with a deep punch into Chet's side, knocking him to the ground. A moan of pain came from Chet's mouth as he curled his body and held his stomach with both hands. Cody, who was more equal in size to Dutch, decided to enter the fray, but Pops held him back, stretching his cane out in front of his oldest son.

"Chet's got to have some pride one way or the other. Let him be," Pops said. The elder Harbison clenched his teeth, hoping he had made the right decision in stopping his older son from putting an end to the fight.

By now both men were rolling in the mud and, much to the dismay of the crowd that was forming around the centerpiece of town, the Spragg boy was winning the battle. Dutch, kneeling in the mud alongside of Chet landed another blow, this time square into his left jaw. Losing his balance after the punch, Dutch picked himself up and staggered back a few paces to evaluate the damage he had done to the much smaller fighter.

Just as nearly everyone thought Chet was done-for, he rolled to his feet and charged an off-balanced Dutch into one of the mules hitched to the hay wagon. The mules lurched and kicked up their rear hooves, missing Dutch's head. As he stood and regained his balance, Dutch reached toward the backside of his belt and returned with a ten-inch hunting knife in his hand. "I'm goin' slice you to pieces soldier boy!"

Dutch turned for a split second after Mrs. Hoffman screamed at the sight of the knife, giving Chet just enough time to grab Dutch's wrist with both hands and then slam his knee high and hard into Dutch's groin. Once wasn't enough as far as Chet was concerned. He now took aim three more times, hitting the target. The big oaf dropped the knife and fell onto his side into a muddy puddle, curling up into such excruciating pain that spectators could only see the whites of his eyes but not his pupils.

"I'll show you how a soldier boy survives in Cuba!" Chet said as he jumped atop of the mud-caked river rat. He clenched his right fist and continually pounded Dutch's face, blow after blow after blow. Within seconds blood was gushing from Dutch's nose, lips and even an ear.

"Enough, Chet, enough old buddy!" Pete shouted as he and Cody pulled him off from the bloody pulp of a man. "You proved your point! You proved your point," Pete repeated.

Chet staggered to his feet, holding his side, coughing and gagging. His nose and his lower lip were bleeding and he had another cut over his right eye. He staggered over to the well in front of Wheeler's and pumped water into one hand held close to his face to get a drink while holding his side with his other hand. After a few gulps, he sat down on the wooden planks of the feed store porch and put his hands up under his chin. He hadn't been this exhausted since San Juan Hill.

Cody and Nelson lifted Dutch out of the mud and leaned him up against a hitching rail post. Pete doused him with a bucket of cold water and the man with the shredded face came-to. After several minutes Cody and Pete let Dutch drink from the horse trough and then lifted the beaten man up onto his horse and handed him the reins.

Cold and wet, and still dazed, Dutch looked down to the wooden walkway and stared at Chet, who was now taking another drink of water, this time from a dipper.

"I'm a wishin' you dead, Harbison, and it's goin' be soon." Then he turned and looked down at Pete. "And that goes for you too, Skinny McKinney!"

"You do all the wishin' you want, river trash," Pete said. "I'm a wishin' the hair on your ass turns into fish hooks on your way back to Cedar Hill, but it don't mean it's ever goin' ta happen!"

Dutch reined the horse to head north at a slow walk. Some in the crowd wondered if the Spragg boy could make it back to his river shanty without falling from the saddle. Nelson felt sorry for him, even though he despised him, and handed him a worn horse blanket to put over his shoulders for warmth. Dutch failed to thank him or even nod to acknowledge Nelson's act of kindness.

"Pete! Please help Cody load the wagon," Byron asked. "I've got to get home and get Helen to look at this busted head of mine. Chet, you're going to have to drive me home. I'm a feelin' a little light-headed."

"Consider it done Mr. Harbison," Pete said. "Cody and I will be seeing you in nothin' flat. I'll help him get it all into the barn as well. And we'll get that buck home for you, too." For once Pete's reply wasn't in his typical bragging style. He meant what he said in a very serious tone.

Everyone, including Chet, knew that the cut on his father's head was a minor and his excuse to not being able to drive the wagon was just a ruse to get his youngest son home to determine if he was hurt. Chet untied Red and led him to the hunting wagon and then tied the reins to a metal ring on the tailgate.

He pushed his father away when the older man attempted to help his son onto the seat of the hunting wagon. "I'm fine Pops, just leave me alone. I'm all right. Just leave me alone!"

After both men managed to get onto the seat, Chet snapped the reins and Prince headed back toward the farm. Red lifted his head once to show his objection, but with Chet at the reins of the wagon the horse decided it might be okay to follow but he didn't like having another horse in front of him.

Nelson, still standing in the muck of the street held muddy dollar bills in his hand, waving his arm to gain Byron's attention to no avail.

"I'll take those back to the farm too," Pete quipped as he grabbed the soiled bills from the shopkeeper.

As the wagon continued down the road to the farm, Red put his ears back and again tried to at least walk alongside the wagon but the reins were too short to accomplish the task.

George Timmons continued to stand in the middle of the muddy road in front of the store as the wagon disappeared over the hill.

"Come on, George," Cody shouted. "Give us a hand loading these oats and then it will probably take all three of us to lift that deer."

HEALING WOUNDS

"Son, I'm awful proud of you stickin' up for me back there, but that push from Spragg was nothin' to fret about," Pops said as he turned his head to look at his bruised son. "Those damn mules push me around more than that when I'm a puttin' them to harness—and you darn well know it. You coulda' killed that poor excuse for a man. He ain't worth goin' to prison for."

"It's more than that," Chet said. "Besides, you probably deserve it when you get shoved by a mule."

They both turned and grinned at each other. But not another word was said for the rest of the ride. Byron wanted to say more but didn't know how to put it into words. Chet wanted to vent about Dutch, but felt there was no need to burden his father with any more than the man had already experienced that day.

As Prince pulled up to the Harbison home, Cody's wife Beth could see all was not well. There was no deer on the back of the hunting wagon, a small bloody scab on Byron's forehead could be seen from the porch, and Chet, coated with a film of dried mud looked what his sister-in-law called "dreadful".

"Momma Helen, come quick!" she said. "Beth rushed to the wagon to help both the men down.

"We're okay!" the two said simultaneously.

"Momma Helen will determine that," Beth scoffed. "You two get into that kitchen and I'll take care of the horses," she said as she started to unhook the trace from the bay. "And don't worry about that long-legged critter of your'n. If I can handle my daddy's Belgium stud horse, I can handle this skinny little thing."

Neither Pops nor Chet were moving fast as they were earlier in the morning. Climbing the four steps of the porch was a real task. Helen stood at the doorway with her hands on her hips looking at the two weathered-looking men.

"Lize, heat up some more water," she said. "You two take off those muddy boots—and Chester, you take off that filthy coat and shirt and whatever else you can without embarrassing our guest.

Callie stood at the back entrance to the kitchen, much the same way as she did the first morning of Chet's arrival. Her jaw hung open. Never had she seen a person in such a wretched state. By now, Lize had put more pots of water on the stove to warm and had fetched clean towels for Chet and Pops. Then she dragged in the metal bathtub and began to fill it with hot water from the stove.

"You two clean yourselves up and then clean up your mess," Helen ordered. "Us women have work outside to tend to." She looked worried but tried not to show it as she ushered Beth, Lize, and Callie out the kitchen door.

Cody, in the wagon, and Pete and George close behind on horseback, arrived about twenty minutes later. Cody drove the two mules through the open overhang of the red barn, watching both sides of the narrow opening.

"Pete, if you'll unhitch the mules, George and I will hang this deer from the center beam where Pops and I can start skinnin' it," Cody said. "We can unload the oats after dinner. Ma ought to have it ready for us soon."

Callie, who had been helping beat the rugs, walked out to the barn to speak with Cody and Pete.

"What in heaven's name happened in town?" she asked Cody.

"Chet, and now Pops, had a run-in with Dutch Spragg," Cody said. "First Spragg called Pops a liar, and then a cripple, but when the bastard—uh, when Spragg pushed Pops to the floor, boy howdy, did the fists fly. Chet was gettin' it bad out in the street from Spragg for the most part, until Dutch pulled a knife on little brother.

"It just made Chet madder than a hornet," Pete chimed in. "You should have seen him, Miss Callie. I think he would have killed that hunk of, uh, trash, if me and Cody hadn't pulled him off."

Cody jabbed Pete with his elbow to let him know enough had been said.

"It just made Chet more determined. Spragg looked like a piece of raw meat after Chet was finished with him," Pete continued despite Cody's subtle advice.

In the kitchen, Pops washed his face off, searched for his pipe and tobacco, and limped to the parlor to be by himself and think. Chet filled the basin with hot water from the stove, washed his face and arms and then removed his muddy clothes and washed the rest of himself while standing in the tub, using the washrag and towels Lize had left for him. With the tub now filled with muddy water, he stepped out of it and rinsed and refilled a hand-washing basin several times before he considered himself to be clean enough to go to his room and rest. His knuckles were bruised to the point of bleeding and one eye was nearly closed shut. After throwing his clothes into a pile on the sun porch he wrapped one towel around his waist and used a dirtier one to wipe up the mud from the kitchen floor. After using a large pot to empty water from the tub and into the sink, he dragged the tub, out the back door, emptying the rest of its contents onto the grass. He was winded from the chore.

As he attempted to climb the steps he cringed from a sharp pain from his abdomen. He looked down to his lower right side and viewed the jagged scar that he brought back with him from Cuba. I've had some hurts before and just like the others this one will go away eventually. The stairs creaked as Chet held onto the arm railing, taking slow steps up to his room on the second floor.

Byron Harbison sat in his favorite chair smoking his corncob pipe, knowing that talking to his youngest son would do no good until the boy had simmered down. Seeing the kitchen was empty, Helen re-entered the house to find her husband.

"What in tarnation is going on with that boy?" Helen asked as she entered the parlor.

"You and I've have met a lot of men who came back from war when we were young'uns. Before they left they were happy-go-lucky. A lot came back with a chunk of a burden on their shoulders, and I'm afraid Chet is one of them from this latest war. I thought he was workin' it out of his system with the help of that skinny horse of his and that pretty girl we've been takin' care of, but he's got a long ways to go.

"Can we at least press charges against that Spragg boy?" Helen asked.

"Not likely. Chet threw the first punch and that other rascal wouldn't even get a slap on the wrist for knockin' me down. He'll get his due someday, just not today."

By now the chores and the information gathering on the part of Callie, Beth, and Lize was over. Beth went upstairs to check on little Cody who was napping. The door to Chet's small room was closed and his sister-in-law was smart enough to leave it that way. Callie and Lize checked the simmering chicken vegetable soup on the stove, and because of the interruption, it was more than finished. Lize added more water to the pot and stirred the mixture that included tomatoes, celery, onions, carrots, and chunks of redskin potatoes.

"I think I'll take a bowl of this up to Chet," Callie said. "He hasn't had anything to eat since breakfast." Lize shook her head with her back turned, but for once, made no suggestions. She didn't want Callie to see the tears in her eyes. The black woman thought of Chester as almost being her son after all of these years.

Being careful not to spill the bowl, Callie tiptoed up the steps and knocked on his door. "Chet, I brought you something to eat."

"Uh, uh, just a minute," he said. With only his clean long-handles on, Chet grabbed a flannel shirt from his bureau and a pair of work pants from the chest by his bed. He felt all of his injuries even more as he bent his arms and legs to get dressed.

"Come on in, I guess."

Chet buttoned his shirt as Callie set the bowl down onto the table next to the kerosene lamp.

"Lize and I just finished making it," she said. "I thought you would be hungry by now—especially with all you've been through. Cody said you did what you did because you had no choice. You had to protect your father?"

"Did they tell you I almost killed Dutch Spragg and that everyone gawking at me thought I was enjoying every second of it—and that I looked like a mad man?"

"No, no he didn't."

"Well that's what I felt," Chet said. "Once I got started I couldn't stop. I thought I was starting to wear the rough off my temper once I started spending time with you, but it all came back."

Callie looked down to the floor.

"Maybe you should talk to someone about it. Talk about what you saw and did when you were fighting with Colonel Roosevelt? Maybe Mr. Frost? He was in the War Between the

States, or maybe you could write to your friend Ritchie that you told me about."

"I don't think Mr. Frost would understand. He came back just fine. And Ritchie, what does he have to fret about? His old man is wealthy and he'll get his son any job he wants to take his mind off of matters."

"Ritchie saw what you saw in Cuba," she said. "He may think you've got it easy coming back to this farm you were probably bragging about."

"Yeah, I guess it wouldn't hurt to write him a letter and see what he's up to and let him know about you."

Chet sipped a spoonful of soup and flinched as the hot broth touched his split lip. He laughed.

"Maybe I should let this cool a bit."

He set the bowl down on the lamp table and walked up to Callie, wrapped his arms around her, and kissed her.

"That kinda hurt my lips, too," he chuckled. "But boy, was it worth it."

Callie kissed him again, this time on his forehead. "Let me know if you want more. I like these sick-call visits."

"More soup, or more kisses?" Chet asked. Callie smiled from ear to ear, turned and walked down the stairs. Then Beth walked past the small bedroom with little Cody in her arms.

"I think I oughta tell Momma Helen about this," she teased.

RED'S RUN

A week passed since the "incident in town" as the Harbison household referred to it. All went back to normal at the farm. The pastures still had some tall but brownish grass and an excellent hay crop resulted in the stud barn loft being full of hay and all the pastures were dotted with haystacks.

Callie walked into the kitchen dressed in her jeans and flannel shirt, grabbing a biscuit and then pouring a cup of coffee. She was greeted by Helen and Lize who were just finishing their own morning meals.

"Where are you off to today?" Helen asked.

"Well if it's all right, I'd like to borrow Buck again to go see Mr. Lee. He and I have sold all the cows we need to, but he still has father's two carriage horses. He said they're not the type of animals that most folks around here need or can afford. The only person who seems interested is Mr. Simpson from the sawmill, but Mr. Lee said he wouldn't buy anything unless it's practically being given away. We're going to work on an advertisement we can put in the St. Louis newspaper— maybe even *The Breeders Gazette and American Stock Farm* magazine out of Chicago.

"You can take Buck today," Helen said, but I'll need him tomorrow for a meeting up at the school. I've been appointed to a head committee about buildin' a proper church in town, which means everyone wants a new building instead of using the schoolhouse but nobody wants to do any of the legwork."

"Yes ma'am," Callie said.

"You better take my work coat from the pantry. There's a cloudbank out to the west and it appears our fall weather has left us for good and winter's going to come in fast today. You know it's almost mid-December. We've been pretty fortunate not to have any snow except for that little bit we had last week.

With the sun shining and the temperature near fifty degrees, Callie doubted that the farm wife's weather prediction would come true, but nonetheless, she took the work coat with her as she walked out the kitchen door.

As she approached the barn to saddle Buck, George Timmons, who had just finished shoeing Rex, the Morgan stallion, greeted Callie.

"Good mornin' Miss Callie. I've been a watchin' you and you sure have come a long way with your ridin'."

"Thanks George," she said. "That's very observant of you. But I'm afraid I've been using Buck too much. My, that's a pretty horse you have there. Do you ride him much?"

George looked down at his boots. "Yes ma'am. Cody and I both do when Rex has, uh, uh, been hired out to other farmers. He's a real smooth ridin' horse, he is."

"I'd love to ride something different," she said. "Buck is a little slow and I know Momma Helen probably wants to use him more but won't come out and say it. Could I ride Rex?"

"Why yes ma'am!" he said, "You sure can!"

George grabbed Buck's gear and began to saddle Rex. He continued to talk with Callie about the weather and anything he could think of. Still talking, he tightened the cinch but neglected to knee the stallion's belly to make sure he wasn't holding in any air. All the while, Pebbles circled the two but neither seemed to notice with Callie admiring the horse and George admiring Callie.

She thanked her friend and rode off at an easy pace. As George had said, Rex had a smooth gait. Pebbles began to follow, but received a stern "Stay home" from Callie, so the spotted dog went back to his favorite spot on the porch.

Moments later Chet, coming from house,' spotted Buck still in the paddock by the red barn.

"Where's Callie? Ma said she was taking Buck to see Mr. Lee."

"Well, she's been ridin' so good she asked to ride Rex," George said, now pausing with a worried look on his face.

Chet shook his head in disbelief. "George, that horse will think he's going to Mr. Lee's to mount mares. He'll go crazy once he turns onto Booger Mountain Road. You know how he gets."

Chet turned to the pasture by the red barn, drew two fingers to his mouth and whistled with all his lungs could muster, and after what seemed like forever he saw Red galloping his way. With the hackamore bridle in hand, Chet placed it on the gelding's head and jumped on his back, galloping off. *I hope this skinny horse can run*, he thought.

As Chet reached the end of the property, he reined in the sorrel enough to tug on the gate's pulley system that Pops had designed to make entering and exiting the farm easy for riders.

Once Chet and Red made it through the gate he pushed his boot heels into Red's flanks. The lanky gelding hadn't felt such a powerful nudge from his current owner, but the animal responded with only a slight jump and started running up the hill to the main road throwing clods of dirt behind his hooves.

Callie continued at an even but somewhat faster pace with Rex as she neared the dirt road that led south to Mr. Lee's place. The canter changed to a gallop and the stallion's ears perks up the closer the animal came to Booger Mountain Road.

By now Chet could see a horse and rider off in the distance and again, with his heels, encouraged his mount to run even faster. Riding bareback was something Chet had performed since he was a small child, and with Red's narrow girth he had excellent control of the beast, but the tighter he wrapped his knees around the animal, the more pain he could feel in his side. It didn't matter. He urged the horse on even more.

Red's wide-open eyes showed a sign of confusion until the long-legged horse tilted his head to notice the black stallion within his vision. Despite the horse already being lathered up, his speed increased. He now understood the urgency of his master's request and there was yet another surge as his hooves devoured the dirt road acting like shovels, throwing chunks of dirt and rock high into the air as his speed increased. Chet's Stetson blew off his head following Red's second surge. The rider tightened his knees around the horse's sides and leaned forward. Holding the reins with just his left hand for a split second, Chet patted the horse's neck to show his approval. Now they both understood their challenge.

Rex's stride picked up even more as Callie reined the animal to turn down the road to Mr. Lee's. *What a confusing name for a road*, she thought, not paying much attention to the increase in the animal's speed. *There is no mountain. It's fairly level, but what is strange is the row of trees farther down on both sides. In the summer and fall the trees block the sunlight completely making it seem like I'm riding through a tunnel. And lately the branches hang so low that I have to duck.*

Returning from her thoughts she realized that Rex was now in what appeared to her to be a full run. She pulled back on the reins to slow the horse but to no avail.

Oh my! She thought. He's not slowing down.

Callie continued to pull the reins back as hard as she could with no results. Rex was now on his own mission—to find some mares. It would be hard for Callie to stop him even if he had the proper bit in his mouth—and he didn't. It was old Buck's headstall.

With a red face and clenched hands Callie jerked at the reins and took up some of the slack, hoping to stop the black brute. But there was no stopping the stallion. He had females on his mind and he knew where he could find them. Callie's heart began to pound and the saddle started to shift from right to left as Rex dodged some of the low hanging branches. "Oh my God, I'm in trouble!"

Then she heard a familiar voice behind her in the distance.

"Callie, let go of the horn! Hold onto the reins and his mane! Hold on as tight as you can!" Chet and Red were more than a hundred yards behind her.

Red's nostrils flared and the horse continued his full stride at an even quicker pace—faster than any horse Chet had ever ridden. The lather from Red's sides began to splatter Chet's face and soak into the thighs of his jeans. Within less than a minute or so Red was only two or three lengths from reaching the stallion. Chet could not believe the speed of the horse that was between his legs.

"Get ready! I'm going to grab you! Get ready!"

Wide-eyed, it seemed like there was no stopping the sorrel horse with his own quest of passing the stallion.

Chet guided Red closer and closer alongside the black stud, which was now in a dead run. Red had run twice the distance at the same speed and showed no signs of fatigue except for his lathered chest.

"You can do it boy! Chet urged. Give it all you got!"

With the horses neck and neck, Chet squeezed his knees as tight as he could and reached for Callie. "Let go! Let go! I've got you!"

Callie leaned to the left as Chet grabbed her waist with his arm and pulled her onto Red. With the tall gelding still at full gallop Callie was now halfway on the horse's back and partially on the lower part of his neck. Rex continued his run, now with only the saddle on his back. He had an urge that would be hard to stop until he found a mare in season.

Callie, with tears of fright falling down her cheek, wrapped her arms around Chet's neck with both legs dangling from Red's side. Neck to neck with Rex, Red now had his own quest—he was determined to pass the other horse no matter how much weight was on his own back—or what his master wanted him to do. Chet's balance was now as awkward as it could be and attempting to rein in had little effect on the sorrel that had performed far beyond Chet's belief.

This damn fool of a horse is still in a race with Rex. He don't want another horse in front of him, Chet thought as he battled to keep Callie and himself on board. And then Red blasted past Rex. There was no stopping him.

Cohen Lee gawked down the lane where he saw the two spirited animals with the youngsters hanging onto the sorrel horse with all their might. The equines were hammering the dirt, heading straight at him and the three horses behind him in the corral. Waving his hands back and forth he attempted to slow Red down as he approached. With Red almost on top of him, Mr. Lee attempted to grab for the horse's bridle but decided it would be better to dive for the dirt and get out of the beast's way. Equally as quick, the gelding lowered his rear legs to stop like he was a cutting horse. The horse's haunches nearly touched the ground and his front legs stretched out in front of him stopping just short of the corral. Chet gripped Red's mane as he lowered Callie to the ground.

Just behind them, Rex imitated the lead horse's actions but crashed his chest into the corral fence, snapping the middle and top rail. His saddle, finally loose, fell to the side and wound up with the seat under his belly. The black stallion, covered with lather, looked confused. There were three geldings behind the fence, Mr. Cavanaugh's two Standard Bred carriage horses and an old swayback grey.

"Chet, I was so scared. He wouldn't stop and I pulled just as hard as I possibly could," Callie sobbed and wrapped her arms around him. He hugged her for several minutes before the crying stopped.

"You did everything you could," he said. "It wasn't your fault." By now Chet was shaking as much as Callie.

"What in tarnation is goin' on?" Mr. Lee asked, picking himself up while he brushed the dirt from his bib overalls.

"George got himself all flustered and decided it was okay to let Callie ride Rex. He didn't take the time to think it over. You know how he can be," Chet said as he staggered over to the stallion. He reached for the mild port bit with the shank turned upwards. "Ol' Rex sure was in a hurry to visit your place," Chet said. "Look, he flipped the bit up in his mouth. Callie couldn't have stopped him no matter how hard she pulled." Then he approached Red and rubbed the horse's forehead with his fist. "Boy, you did a fine job. I didn't know you had it in you, but I should have replaced your hackamore weeks ago with something more substantial. I'm not sure if even that old bicycle bit would have stopped you today!"

"I had a big saddle horse kinda' like that red one of yours when I was younger," Mr. Lee quipped. "He was a strawberry roan, and he wouldn't ever let another animal lead the way. Yep, old Bob, he was one of the few horses I ever owned that never went up for sale."

Mr. Lee turned to see the expression on Chet's face. Instead, he saw the young man's ashen complexion just before Chet's knees buckled and he collapsed to the ground.

"Oh my God, he's bleeding!"

Callie knelt down to his side. "Chet, wake up, wake up!"

The lower half of Chet's shirt and his jeans were soaked with blood.

Then he forced his eyes open and looked into Callie's. "I'll be okay. I just need to rest a bit," he said as he passed out for a second time.

"Dolly's already hitched up to the mail wagon in the barn," Mr. Lee said. "You need to get him back home. I'll tie these two fellas to the back of the wagon and throw the black's saddle onto that old crow bait in the corral and ride over to Wheeler's to call Doc Bockelman. Callie, you take it real easy gettin' back to the Harbisons."

The two lifted Chet onto the wagon seat and Mr. Lee handed his big red handkerchief to Chet. "Hold this tight against your wound, son. The doc will be at your place in an hour or so if I can get him on the phone. Helen will know what to do in the meantime."

Within minutes of the start of their trip back home, the storm began to move in. The wind picked up and Callie and Chet were pelted, first by rain and then by sleet. As the mail wagon rolled up to the Harbison farm Chet was leaning heavily on Callie's shoulder. Callie had used Helen's coat as a blanket to keep him warm.

"Help! I need help! Chet's hurt!" Callie called.

Cody and Beth ran from the house. George arrived on the scene first from the corral and was already holding Dolly's bridle to keep the wagon from moving.

"Chet, Miss Callie, I done wrong. I caused this and I am so sorry," George said.

Chet looked up, barely conscious. "It's okay George. It's all okay."

With one arm around Cody and the other around Beth, Chet attempted to walk to the house

Chet turned his head back to George. "Take care of Red and Rex."

Then he slumped down, falling to his knees. Cody grabbed his brother with both arms and carried him the rest of the way to the house, scurried through the kitchen and hallway and gently placed him onto the bed in Callie's room. By now, Helen was tearing up sheets to wrap around the wound on Chet's lower left side. Callie sat on the leather couch next to her bed and sobbed as she watched the man she loved wracked with pain.

"This would have never happened if I hadn't asked George to ride that other horse," she said. "It wasn't his fault. It was all mine."

Snow began to cover the ground within the next hour when Dr. Clifford Bockelman arrived. He stepped down from his rig and then leaned back in to reach for his large worn leather satchel. He tied his horse to the hitching rail and then took his steps slowly along the stone walk that led to the kitchen door. Pops greeted him holding the screen door open. Lize reached to help him with his coat and hat.

"He's hurt bad Doc," Pops said. "His gut is torn open and he's bleeding."

"Byron, I'll give him a good looking over and then we'll take care of him," he assured.

The doctor, who was pushing seventy years old, was slender in build, but over the years had developed an old-man's pouch for a stomach. He was about five feet, seven inches tall, but his slumped shoulders made him look shorter. His thin hair was parted down the middle and a pair of wire-rimmed spectacles that rested halfway down his nose framed his clean-shaven face.

"Let's get a look at the patient," he said as he rolled up his sleeves.

As the doctor entered the room, a weakened Chet looked up, "Hi Dr. Bockey." It was a name he and Cody had used since they could talk, because as youngsters neither could pronounce his name.

Bockelman gave a grin and then began to cut the bandages loose with a pair of scissors from his medical bag. "Hmph" was the only sound coming from the doctor as he poked and prodded during his examination. He didn't have to ask Chet if it hurt. He could see the agonizing look on the young man's face every time he attempted to get a closer look inside the injured abdomen.

"Son, this is more than a wound. It's all infected in there and I'm going to have to find out what it is. It's going to be very painful—more than it is now, so I'm going to put you out with some ether. Do you know what that is?"

Chet nodded and Bockelman ordered Lize to boil some water to soak the forceps and scalpel he would use.

Two hours later, as Dr. Bockelman finished with stitches he looked up at Helen and Byron. "Think a man could get a cup of coffee around here? Chet will be coming out of it soon and we'll all talk. I need to stretch my legs after this. Let's go to the kitchen. Callie, you keep an eye on this young man for us."

As Bockelman finished his second cup of coffee, he heard what he had predicted.

"Doctor! Chet's awake," Callie said.

Helen and Byron followed him to the bedroom, while Lize, Cody, Beth, and Little Cody stayed nearby in the hallway.

Chet lay flat on his back with his eyelids only half open.

"Son, I'm sure that Army surgeon did as good job as he could sewing you up out in the jungle, but he missed something in that wound. What was it from—a knife?"

"Bayonet," Chet whispered.

"Well, he missed a small piece of metal—probably the tip of the blade," Bockelman said as he held up a speck of metal up with a pair of forceps. "Under normal circumstances this little piece of rust probably would have stayed encased in scar tissue and you would have hardly noticed it. But from what your pa has been telling me you probably stirred it loose with your barroom brawlin' and street fightin'. My guess is that today's act of trying to be Prince Charming, rescuing your damsel in distress was the straw that broke the camel's back and that hunk of metal finally tore through your gut. That bout with malaria hasn't helped you any either."

Chet grinned and Callie blushed.

"I don't want you moving from this bed for a couple of weeks. And I don't want you out of this house until at least February. Your ma and these other women of the house are going to have to clean that wound once or twice a day. And I'm leaving you with a bottle of laudanum for pain. You're only to take a spoonful once in the morning and once at night. Do you understand?"

"Yeah, Doc. Anything else?" Chet asked.

"Well you're too big for me to give you a nickel for being a good patient, and I know your folks have always been good about paying their bills, but I do have a request for you and your brother. Come this spring I want you to pick out a good buggy horse for me. Copper is going on 16 years old and these trips all over the countryside from Dittmer are getting a little tough for him—and me too. Pick me a good one. I know a widow with two kids down the road from me that could benefit from Copper. Their old plug is about ready for the glue factory. I think he can make it through until spring—I've been tending to critters almost as much as I have people lately."

"I'll stop back next week. I'd better get home before that snow gets any deeper."

HEALING

The next morning, Helen Harbison walked into the room where her youngest son lay. There she saw Callie sitting in a chair close-up to the bed, holding Chet's hand.

"How's he doing dear?" Helen asked.

"He's still got a fever and he's been pretty restless all night," she said. "He slept best after taking that medicine the doctor gave him. He'll be due for some more soon."

"We need to get some broth in his stomach first," Helen said. "Even if he's not hungry. Why don't you try to get some rest yourself? You're not going to be any good to him if you get sick too. I put clean sheets on his bed upstairs. Go up and get some rest."

"Yes ma'am," she said, too tired to argue. She pulled herself out of the chair and walked up the steps to Chet's room. She fell to the bed and closed her eyes, exhausted from the day and night before.

For the next week Callie, Helen, Beth, and Lize tended to Chet—feeding him, cleaning and rewrapping his wound as well as his other needs.

"He's doing much better today," Callie said as Helen entered the room.

Chet look up and smiled at his mother. "I'm going to be fine, Ma, especially with all the treatment you gals have given me. I just want to get out of this bed."

"Not until the doctor says so," Callie said. "He's coming back tomorrow to take the stitches out. But until then, you stay put."

Helen nodded in agreement. "I've got to get breakfast going for the men. I think Chet's ready to eat something more solid than mush by now."

"And we've got to get you cleaned up today," Callie said. "You've got company coming. Lize forbade Pete and George from seeing you when you were so sick, but she and your momma have decided you're up to it. I'll be right back."

Callie returned minutes later with as small pan of hot water, soap, and a washcloth. "Let's start with cleaning your wound—it's just about healed—and then we'll see if you can shave yourself or if I need to do it."

"I'm better now. I can do that myself," Chet said. "Really, I can."

Not paying any attention to his comment, Callie pulled the sheet away to do what she and Helen had been doing for the past week."

"Oh! Uh, uh, I guess you are feeling better," she said, with her face turning red but smiling at the same time. "You've shown a 'big' improvement overnight!"

Chet's face was equally red, but he had a broader smile. "Yep, I'm feelin' as healthy as a horse or maybe even ol' Samson out in the barn… or Goliath at the Miller place."

Callie's face turned an even darker shade of red.

"You heard Beth and me talking up in the hayloft that day? How embarrassing."

Then she smiled and threw the washcloth at his face.

"I think you're feeling good enough to shave yourself, too," she said.

Then she kissed him on the lips.

"I have some cleaning up to do as well if the boys are coming in to see you. I can't be seen like this. My hair is a mess and I need to change clothes. I will see you later... Mr. Goliath!"

George Timmons and Pete McKinney arrived at the Harbison place at the same time.

"You boys don't go gettin' little Chester all excited, and I better not find out that you brought any corn liquor into this house," Lize said. "Do you understand?"

"Yes ma'am," Pete said with a glint in his eye.

"I would never, never do that Miz Lize," George said.

Callie was sitting in the chair next to Chet's bed when the two walked in, followed by Cody. George stood at the door apologetically as Pete threw himself onto the leather couch, leaned back, crossed his legs and relaxed.

"Chet, Miss Callie, I'm just so sorry I caused all of this pain for you two," George said.

"George, it was just an honest mistake, and the doc says this would have happened anyway with all the work I do on the farm. You just helped me get it over with sooner, that's all."

"Oh, enough of that," Pete said. "Let's start a talkin' about the Fourth of July race up at Hillsboro. Are you goin' be well enough to ride that tall drink of water of a horse of yours while Cody and I place the bets in the stands? From what Mr. Lee and Callie tell me that horse of your'n can outrun anything around here. We could really clean up, just like we did in ninety-six and ninety-seven."

"What in heaven's name are you talkin' about?" Callie asked.

Chet grinned. "A few years back we had a mule filly that was foaled by one of our fastest Morgan mares and good ol' Samson. Anyway, Hillsboro has that big fair every summer and we all knew this mule could whip any four-legged critter around but we weren't so sure we could get anybody to bet against her if they saw how good she looked.

"We practiced racing her with other horses on the farm all spring and took extra special care not to let anybody know about it," Chet said. "Instead of trimming her mane, we let it grow out and never ran a brush through it or her tail. The day before the show, we let her roll in the muddiest puddle we could find and then saddled her up with an old beat-up saddle that Pete found in his grandpa's barn. The only thing new on it was the cinch.

"It was decided that since Pete was the scrawniest of us that he would be the jockey. When the horses were all out on the track, me and Cody started talkin' to the menfolk in the stands where the bettin' took place. We moved from row to row sayin' we just felt sorry for that hayseed farmer kid—Pete wasn't exactly wearin' his Sunday go-to-meetin' clothes—and we were puttin' our money on him and that worthless lookin' mule.

"Just about everybody bet us a quarter or fifty cents, thinking we were crazy," Chet said. "As fast as that filly was, and as skinny as Pete was, that mule should have taken the lead as soon as the starting pistol was fired, except we didn't think about that mule bein' scared of gunfire. She reared up and almost dumped Pete to the ground. But to give Pete credit, he calmed her down and took off down the track eatin' everyone's dust. But by the time they finished that race around and about the fairgrounds, Betsy and Pete were in the lead by nearly five lengths.

"We went home with nearly fifty bucks between the three of us but didn't do nearly as good in ninety-seven—by then a lot of folks had figured out what we had done and nobody wanted to bet against us."

"So what you say Chet, are you goin' race Red this summer? I've been lookin' him over real good and I can start helpin' ya' work 'im when you a feelin' better."

"Naw!" Chet said. "A horse like him—I don't want him getting' all kicked up by those plow jockeys who think they're cowboys. After last week Red don't have to prove nothin' to nobody—after all, he saved my gal! I already know he's the best. Besides, half the people in the county know what happened. I've been gettin' get-well letters from folks I haven't seen or heard from in years."

Cody stood in the doorway with his arms folded and a smirk on his face.

"Little brother, when Pete says he's been lookin' over Red, he does mean 'over.' He walked over to the paddock the other day thinkin' he was goin' walk Red back to his stall and saddle him up. Your sawed-off little friend grabbed that halter a little too quick and ol' Red threw his head back so fast he lifted Pete into the air and flipped him like a flapjack. Pops was there and I'd never seen him laugh so hard in my entire life.

"The fact of the matter is that Red's partial to only a few people," Cody said. "I can put him up in the stall and feed him, but I tried to saddle him up Friday and he wouldn't have anything to do with it.

"Ma saw what was goin' on and said me and Pete were acting too much like rough necks," Cody said. "It seems she and little Callie here are havin' the best luck with him. They haven't tried to ride him, but that damn, uh darn, horse will let them do anything as far as cleanin' his hooves, brushin' him, and leadin' him around the paddock. Heck, with what Callie's been doin', maybe she or Ma should enter him in the race and you can take bets in the stands."

Chet's mouth hung open.

Callie blushed and shook her head. "Momma Helen's been showing me a lot about horses while you've been resting, but after the other week I don't want to be a part of any horse race—one was enough for me."

CHORES & CHALLENGES

A week later Chet was feeling better but still had orders to take it easy and continue bed rest. Farm work continued with George and Pete helping as much as they could. It was time for another Harbison trip to St. Louis, a trip that would make paying bills through the spring possible.

"Don't worry. With Lize here to help, we can handle just about anything that needs to be handled," Callie said. "Besides, you'll be back in a few days."

"I just don't know about leaving you two here with all the chores to do and Chet still being laid up in bed," Helen said.

"Helen, you know that even though she's a city gal Callie can handle feedin' the horses and the chickens, and Lize can handle the cooking," Pops said. "Cody, George, and Pete are already up to the road with those strings of mules we have to get to the dairy for Tom Langer. Besides, we promised Margie that Beth and little Cody would be comin' along on the next trip."

"Byron, that filly in the barn is going to foal soon. What if she has some trouble?"

"Wheeler and Cohen are just up the road. All Callie has to do is saddle up Buck and fetch them."

With that, Helen Harbison joined her husband on the front seat of the buggy, while Beth and little Cody shared a blanket on the seat behind them.

"Come on Prince! Let's go Spike! We got some catchin' up to do," Pops said as he snapped the reins.

Callie and Lize waved as the buggy drove off. They felt a stiff breeze from the west. "Get yourself inside and get a coat before you start your outdoor chores," Lize ordered.

After grabbing Momma Helen's barn coat from the pantry, Callie poked her head inside the door to where Chet lay resting. "I'm going to be out feeding the chickens and the horses, but Lize is here if you need anything."

"I'll be fine," Chet said. "You know I've been feelin' good enough to make it to the outhouse lately. I could walk along with you."

"Oh no you don't!" Callie said. "Doctor Bockelman said that going to the privy was plenty of exercise and he didn't want you over exerting yourself with anything else. And when you need to go out there, you don't do it unless Lize or I walk you out."

"Yes Ma'am, I'll stay right where I am—but make sure you keep Red's stall clean until I'm up to it," he said with a grin.

Callie turned her head and strutted from the door entrance. She grabbed the wicker basket on the kitchen floor and headed outside for the hen house. The chickens sprang from their nesting boxes as she filled the feeder with grain, and once they all reached the floor she searched the nesting boxes for fresh brown eggs.

As cold as it is, I'm surprised the hens are laying as many eggs as they are. By the time she was done she had found seven eggs in the dozen nesting boxes that lined the wall. After returning to the kitchen to deposit the eggs, she went back outside to the barn to milk the cow. She had been getting the hang of the new chore for the past couple of weeks, but her hands and fingers were hurting by the time the bucket was full.

Feeding the horses was no big chore for Callie. Wooden grain boxes were nailed in place by the front of each stall, and each one had a manger for hay. Red, Buck, and the other six horses in the barn perked up when they heard Callie enter. Oats were stored in an oak barrel in the barn's hallway with a large stone sitting on top of the lid. Next to the barrel one of the farm's nearly feral cats could be found perched on a railing, almost eager to see Callie.

"You old cat, I don't know why they keep you mean little critters around this place," she said, knowing the animal would not allow her to pet it.

The cat continued to look at the barrel but purred back to Callie's comments.

Callie lifted the stone from the lid, flipped it open and reached inside with her right hand to find the metal scoop. As she did the cat attacked her—at least that's what Callie thought was taking place as she jumped back in shock. In what seemed like a split second, a gray rat ran up the girl's arm and within another split second, the cat had trounced the rodent and was ripping it to shreds with its claws and teeth.

All eight horses jerked and backed into the barn walls as Callie screamed at the top of her lungs. When it was all over she realized that the cat was waiting for her dinner, just like the horses were. Callie looked inside the barrel before reaching in, saw it was free of rodents and proceeded to fill the scoop with oats. By now Callie, and the horses, were calmed down. She filled their feed boxes and then grabbed the pitchfork and put hay in each of their mangers.

Then came the hard part. With winter in full swing, the nearby pond had frozen. Part of her chores included taking an ax and chopping a big enough hole into the ice for the horses and mules to get water. Cody had been thoughtful enough to handle the chore for Callie's Angus cattle up the road before he left, as well as feeding and watering the stallions. She would not have to venture across the creek or to her father's land to perform that duty again until tomorrow.

Once the ice was broken, she took on the two jobs she liked the least: "packing" buckets of water, one at a time, back to the barn for the horses, and shoveling out the stalls. Each trip to and from the pond took at least five minutes. With snow on the ground it took longer. Although Chet and Cody could manage two buckets at a time, one was a struggle for the girl who weighed less than a hundred pounds. That meant eight long trips. She was glad she had remembered to wrap a scarf around her head and to wear Chet's leather work gloves.

Then Callie took on the task of pushing an empty wooden wheelbarrow through the barn hallway, stopping at each stall. Cody had told her that the chore could wait until he returned, but she remembered how both Chet and Cody almost bragged about cleaning the stalls every day. Once there, she'd grab the broad and flat shovel and begin picking up the half-frozen manure-and-straw-mix and dump it into the wheelbarrow. Once the wheelbarrow was full she rolled it out to the barn's lean-to that sheltered the manure spreader. Shoveling from the wheelbarrow to the back of the spreader was almost as hard as packing water but Callie had the job done within a short period of time. She knew that the wagonload of horse droppings and rotted straw would help Momma Helen's garden, as well as the farm pastures, produce a healthier crop and pasture next spring.

She shuffled the soles of her rubber boots along the snow-covered ground as she pushed the wheelbarrow back inside the barn. She wanted to get as much of the manure off before she got back to the house so she wouldn't have to scrape them as much. As she placed the wheelbarrow up along the barn wall in the hallway she noticed that the dark-gray filly had not touched her feed even though all the other horses had nearly completed their meal. The horse, whose abdomen was quite pronounced, seemed restless, walking back and forth in her stall. When Callie tried to pet her, the horse backed away in a skittish manner.

Something's not right. I better ask Chet about this.

As she stood in the entranceway to her former room, Chet answered her questions.

"It's pretty common for a first-time momma to act like that," Chet said. "Pops didn't think she would foal at least for another week, but Mother Nature decides that. Most of the time they seem to have their young'uns after dark. You probably ought to check on her every hour or so, and again just before you go to bed. Heck, I'm feelin' fair to middlin', why don't I put a coat on and go out there and take a look-see?"

"You'll do no such thing!" Callie said. "I'm just as much responsible as George for you being in the condition you're in. I told your mother and father I can handle this. Besides, Lize can help me."

Chet straightened up and adjusted his pillows as he let out a laugh.

"You can get Lize to ring a chicken's neck so we can have it for supper and she'll even get a garden hoe and go to the spring house by her lonesome for butter and cream even when someone's seen snakes by it, but don't expect her to help you with the horses or the mules. She's afraid of them. Pops said she's been that way ever since she was a little girl."

"Well you never mind about Lize," Callie said. "If something has to be done, you just tell me how to do it. Besides, I can always ride Buck up to get Mr. Frost."

"Maybe not," Chet said as he looked out the window. "Take a look at that snow. It's coming down so hard I can hardly see the outhouse from here. I sure hope it's not this bad on the road up to St. Louis.

"Look, don't worry, maybe she won't have that little filly or fella until everyone gets back," Chet said.

On his insistence, Chet was allowed to move to the leather couch in his makeshift hospital room to eat his supper. Even then his conversation with Callie turned to a terse discussion on terms to define mealtime.

"Eat your dinner," Callie said. "Lize really worked hard on that today because she said chicken and dumplings are your favorite."

"I'm enjoyin' it, but it ain't dinner," Chet said. "I had dinner just after noon. This is supper."

"I'm starting to get used to farm life, other than the rats and the manure shoveling," Callie quipped, "but I just don't understand the way you call some of the things you do around here. You 'pack' water instead of hauling it and a 'grass widder' is a woman who's been divorced. Cody says he's in "high-cotton" when the only thing out in the pasture is tall grass, and now you're telling me that that plate full of food in front of you isn't dinner?"

Chet just laughed again, this time holding his side to keep it from hurting. "Look Callie. I love you more than anything—even if YOU talk a little funny. You'll get better at it."

"Oh my!" She said after she heard him use the word "love" for the first time. "I guess I will."

Chet's face turned blank when he saw the angelic expression on Callie's face.

What did I say now? He thought.

"Let's finish 'supper,'" she said. "I have to check on that filly."

Now bundled in Momma Helen's heaviest winter work coat with a lantern in hand, Callie returned to the barn. Her troubles with a rat and a cat earlier in the day had escaped her—after all, Chet said he loved her more than anything else in the world. Reality kicked in once again as she raised the lantern as high as she could to check on the gray filly. To her surprise, the birth had taken place while Callie was having her "supper" with Chet. The bad news was that the foal's mother would have nothing to do with him. Still covered with part of the afterbirth, every time the colt tried to suckle from its mother, the filly would back away, and even try to kick. She acted as if her offspring was a coyote instead of horse. Callie ran back to the house as fast as she could.

"She's never had a foal before. Sometimes they'll reject 'em." Chet explained. "You're going to have to try and get her to accept him. On the floor of the stall you'll see the afterbirth. The vet calls it a placenta. Take some of the slimy stuff into your hands and rub it on the colt's nose and mouth. Don't wear any gloves. You don't want them to smell leather. You want them to smell the stuff you're putting on. Then take some more and rub some on the momma's udders. Her bag has dropped by now and it will kind a look like the udders on a cow. Smear it all over them and then see if she'll accept the little guy."

Following Chet's exact orders, she rushed to the barn, entered the stall and knelt down and filled her hands with the substance that seemed to be floating on top of the straw and proceeded with Chet's instructions. But it didn't work. In addition, it made Callie so nauseated she almost threw up. She forced herself to breathe through her mouth. It helped, a little.

Every time the colt approached her mother, the mare turned away and began to kick. Once, she even clipped the colt's snoot. It was hard to tell who was more traumatized— the colt, the mare, or Callie.

"We're running out of options," Chet said on Callie's return to his room. "I want you to pick up as much of the afterbirth as possible and put it on the foal's back. Rub it all over him. It might work.

But it didn't.

Callie again, stood in front of her boyfriend, her coat, jeans and hands still smeared in muck from the foal. Some of it was even in her hair. Chet knew not to comment on her appearance, although he thought to himself, *I guess this gal really does love me. Lori Simpson wouldn't even go to the henhouse to fetch eggs.*

"Let me go with you to the barn," Chet said. "I'll be real careful, and I'll tell you what to do. The only other choice we have is to go to the south pasture and bring in Goldie and her foal. Goldie's been with us a long time and she's been willing to nurse two foals at one time if a mare has died during birthing. You wouldn't be able to find her until after sunrise, and I don't think that little fellow in the barn can last that long."

"No! You're staying put. In fact, you're not even going out to the privy," she said, looking at the bedpan, barely underneath the bed frame. "There's more than a foot of snow out there now and it's turning to freezing rain. Tell me what to do. I can do it."

"It's a trick I learned from Mr. Langer at the dairy," Chet said. "First, put a halter on the filly and tie her up to the stall post where she can't hardly move her head. On the same wall we hang the bridles there's a set of leather hobbles—kinda' like handcuffs for horses. Strap them onto the mother's front feet, and be careful. She's going to be jumpy as it is. Now this is the hard part—"

"Gee, I didn't catch the easy part!" Callie said.

"Take a lariat hanging from the same wall and loop it around the mother's left rear ankle," Chet said. "Run the other end of the rope through one of the rings on the halter. Take up all the slack, forcing her to raise that left rear leg really high. She won't like it, but she won't be able kick the foal or you because she'd fall trying to lift the other rear leg, and she's hobbled in the front. Then see if the little fella can do the rest."

Callie's winter coat seemed too cumbersome for her next task, so after reaching the barn she removed it and went about her duties following Chet's exact orders. She wrapped her arms around the foal, lifted and nearly forced it to be near its confused mother. She also learned from Chet that the mare's name was Milly, and Milly the filly, did not take kindly to the short tying up of her halter, the hobbles she had never worn before, or the Scotch-hobble technique that Mr. Langer had shown to Chet while doctoring Red in St. Louis. But Callie made it work. Then she plopped down onto some clean straw in the corner of the stall, leaned back, exhausted, and waited. Pebbles came to her side and nuzzled her.

Sure enough, it worked. The foal began to suckle and Milly couldn't kick. As time went by the mare calmed down. After a time, the colt appeared satisfied and lay down to rest. Callie removed the Scotch hobble and loosened the lead rope slightly before leaving the barn. She knew she'd have to be back in a couple of hours and tighten up the ropes again, just to make sure the foal could nurse.

After taking his medicine Chet had dozed off for only a few minutes when Callie burst into his room and kissed him on his lips.

"It worked! Everything you told me to do this time worked," she said. "You're sure not that dumb reckless 'hayseed' Father used to call you."

"Thanks, I guess," Chet said, somewhat puzzled at the remark. He tried not to notice the mess Callie had brushed onto his blanket from her shirt. He had to turn his head to get away from the smell.

"I guess that's not some of that fancy lilac water you usually wear," he said with a grin as he intentionally twitched his nose.

"Oh, I'm so sorry dear," she said. "I'll have Lize bring you a clean blanket. But don't you dare open this door after she closes it. I can't wait until Saturday night bath night. I've got to take a bath now. Don't you dare try peeking into the kitchen!"

Chet held his right hand over his eyes and then spread his fingers out so his eyes were no longer covered. "I promise," he said with a broad smile on his face. "You can trust me."

CHRISTMAS ON THE FARM

The Harbisons made it back to the farm, although a day late because of the snow, and were amazed at the story Lize had to tell about "Miss Callie tendin' to the filly and colt like she was raised on a farm as a child."

"You musta done a fine job," Pops said. "I ain't heard Lize compliment hardly a sole acceptin' when that McKinney boy promises he's finally going home, and then finally goes."

Cody had chopped down the nicest Christmas tree he could find on the farm and brought it into the parlor after cleaning the branches of dead leaves and brush. Helen and Lize placed it in a bucket of wet sand to hold the tree upright. Callie and Beth strung popcorn onto it while Little Cody watched as he was warned not to touch.

"This Christmas is bittersweet with Mother, Father, and Agnus all gone," Callie said. "But I can't think of anyone else I would rather be with then all of you," she said as they gathered in the parlor on Christmas Eve to open gifts. "And I'm so thankful Chet is better. Just having him walk around the house doing normal things—it's a miracle after how bad he was hurt."

Little Cody got more presents than anyone, but his favorite was a rocking mule made by his father. The child was still too young to rock the equine by himself, but Beth held him on the seat as his father gently rocked the long-eared animal back and forth to the child's delight.

Helen was presented with a new batch of fabric and sewing supplies; Pops received different cans of pipe tobacco from almost everyone in the family; and Lize got a new dress that she had been eying up at Nelson's store. Store-bought clothes were a special treat for her.

Callie presented Chet with a large box wrapped in tissue paper with a bright green ribbon wrapped around it. While not a total surprise, it was an appreciated gift—a wide-brimmed Stetson, almost identical to the one Chet had lost in his race on Red to rescue her.

"I still wonder what happened to that other hat," he said as he tried the new one on for size. "My guess is it got covered with snow and then trampled to bits by some team of horses."

"One of them Spraggs probably found it and is wearin' it now, or maybe a teamster going by got it," Cody said.

"Let's not ruin Christmas talking about those horrible individuals," Callie said. "Chet there's more in the box for you."

Chet reached into the bottom of the hatbox and found a leather-bound copy of A Connecticut Yankee in King Arthur's Court, written by Mark Twain. He was impressed. The book even had an illustration of a knight in shining armor atop his steed.

"I had a copy of the book at home before the, uh, fire. It didn't have the word 'Connecticut' in the title in that issue. Mr. Nelson did a lot of checking before he found where he could order it. It came all the way from New York. It's about a Prince Charming, just like you," Callie said.

Chet blushed.

Callie looked at all the opened presents on the floor, but none were from Chet to her. She acted as if she didn't notice, but Chet knew better.

"Ma wouldn't let me bring your present into the parlor," Chet joked. "You'll have to put your coat on and come out to the blacksmith shed to see it."

With his new white Stetson on his head and a winter coat that his mother had insisted he wear, Chet held Callie's hand with one and steadied himself with one of Pops' canes in the other. The lantern was already lit in the shed. As Chet opened the door Callie saw a dapple-gray mare with white socks and a blaze down its face.

"This is Ashes," Chet said. "She's five years old and she was my personal horse before I left to join Colonel Roosevelt," he said. "Cody turned her into a broodmare, but now that the colt has been weaned, I've been havin' George workin' with her down in the bottoms where you couldn't see them. She's plenty gentle thanks to all the work he's been doin'. Poor ol' George is still feelin' guilty about the whole ordeal even though Cody and me have told him otherwise. She's real gentle, but she's got a might more spirit than old Buck, but not nearly as much as Rex."

Then he walked her over to a homemade saddle stand with a brand new saddle on top of it.

"This is called a basket-weave design," he said as he pointed to imbedding on the saddle that also had "Callie" engraved in the leather. "I ordered it from a friend of mine in Poplar Bluff. He's got a daughter just about your size so the seat should fit you perfectly."

"She's beautiful and the saddle is very pretty," Callie said quietly.

"You'd better look that saddle over really close before we go in," he said.

The redheaded girl walked up closer to the saddle and spotted a leather pouch tied to the horn. She untied it and emptied the contents into her other hand—two gold bands, one with a small diamond chip encased in it.

"Mr. Lee helped me find it. He had a whole bunch of catalogs we looked through while you were out with Beth," he said. "With all this snow, I didn't think it would get here. But it did, just yesterday.

"I was a hopin' you'd marry me this spring after I'm up and about, and the new church is done," he said. "Once I start feelin' a little better, Ma's probably goin' to want to farm you out down the road to keep us apart, since I'm a goin' be feelin' my oats about you real strong by then," he laughed. "There's a little cabin down the main road that I can rent until I get back on my feet and start earnin' some real money. Lize tells me the upstairs got pretty noisy after Beth and Cody got hitched. And there ain't enough room upstairs for both of us unless Lize moves into my little room. And that ain't goin' to happen. She calls it her own personal castle—don't hardly let anyone in except little Cody. I haven't been in there since I was little."

"Yes! Yes, I will marry you," she said with tears falling down her cheeks. "And I'll live anywhere you want us to, even if it's in the barn." She wrapped her arms around her man and kissed him. "And I thought all you had gotten me was a horse!"

"Gee, I thought the horse was the best part," Chet said. "I figured you already knew I wanted to get hitched to you."

SLITHERING SNAKES

Chet looked out the kitchen window, watching the morning sunrise with Callie at his side. Yellow jonquils lined the stone walkway to the road in front of the farmhouse.

"I've never been more happy to see spring," he said. "The pastures are greenin' up after all the snow and rain we've had, and nearly all the broodmares are with foals, and I'm finally back to where I can earn my keep around here."

"And we're getting married in just a little more than two months," Callie chimed in as she squeezed Chet's hand. "We'll be the first couple to be married in the new church."

The two, hand in hand, walked out to the porch and then strolled out to get a look at how the overnight rain had given the farm a look of revitalization—and had helped improved their faith in the world as well.

"Are you sure you're up to riding?" Callie asked as she and Chet continued their walk to the paddock. "Maybe you should start with Buck."

"I'm fine and Red will do just fine. George helped me shoe him yesterday and he was as calm as can be and ready to ride," he said. "I owe that to you and Ma for taking such good care of him while I was laid up.

"Doc Bockey said I am shipshape too. I've been nursed enough. It's time to get to work. Besides, that heavy rain we had the past couple of days caused the creek to overflow down in the bottoms and the rush of water and brush busted all the barbed wire loose. We've got four yearling mules missing. Cody and Pete left early and are out lookin' for 'em. George is out of town. Mr. Frost asked him to go over to Luebbering to help some old widder woman and her pa. That storm blew part of the cedar shakes off the roof of their house, and more rain's a comin'. He's been spendin' a lot of time up there ever since. I guess that roof is in pretty sad shape. Anyway, it's about time for me and Red to get some work done. And who could ask for a better day in the middle of March? The thermometer that Mr. Lee gave Ma and Pops says it's pushin' seventy degrees—strange weather, but I'll take it."

"Okay, but you better be careful," Callie said. "Our wedding is set for the middle of May and I don't want to see you coming down the aisle on crutches because you started playing cowboy too soon. I would go with you but we have to go up to Mr. Nelson's to pick up the fabric we ordered for the wedding dress. It's going to be beautiful. You should come with us."

"Uh, I love you dearly, but that type of chore better suits you, Ma, Beth, and Lize. I'll be careful."

The two hugged and kissed, and then Chet placed two fingers in his mouth and whistled. The familiar sound caused Red's ears to perk up and he trotted to the gate of the paddock knowing that an apple or some other treat would be waiting for him—and just maybe a saddle and bridle.

"Boy, he sure has put some weight on over the winter," Chet said. "He's had his share of oats and hay without much exercise."

"Now that's not true," Callie said. "Mother Helen and I have had him on a lunge line, working him in the paddock to stay in shape for you. We even got him used to wearing that sturdier hackamore you ordered for him. It's all the green grass he's been eating lately. It seems like he didn't know what real grass was at first, but once he saw the other horses eating it there was no stopping him. He looks filled out now like the Morgans."

"Probably never had much fresh pasture before I acquired him," Chet said. "We may have to watch him so he doesn't eat too much. We don't want him to founder."

After Red took a lump of sugar, Chet put on his bridle, making sure it was not too tight of a fit. The blanket and saddle followed, with Chet noticing that the marks on the cinch from tying the knot last fall and winter didn't match up with part of the leather strap where the knot was now tied. Red had gained at least fifty pounds, and looked the better for it.

"You're wearing your gun belt today," Callie said. "You don't think the Spragg boys had anything to do with the missing mules do you?

"It's not likely they would have been out in the storm last night and the river just might be too high to cross for a while," Chet said. "We've had a lot of coyotes out here with the warm weather, though. Old man Hoffman lost one of his calves because of them varmints. I'm just takin' it as a precaution.

Chet kissed his bride-to-be one more time and mounted the gelding. It was a good feeling for Chet. For the first time in months there were no sharp pains—just a little stiffness. Red must have felt pretty good himself—his ears remained pointed straight up, not back like they were when the two first met on the cobblestone streets of downtown St. Louis.

That fat-assed peddler probably wouldn't even recognize Red if he saw him now, Chet thought. *If I hadn't stopped at Glen's for that haircut this ol' boy probably would be in a glue factory by now. And that would have been a tragic waste of horseflesh.*

Mr. Langer will be pleased when he sees him at the wedding, Chet thought to himself. But he'll be even more impressed when he and Mrs. Langer meet Callie.

Chet kept Red at a steady walk as the two experienced their first journey of the year. He only urged the horse on when they were forced to climb the steep and muddy embankment after crossing the flowing creek.

Just as Cody had explained, the fence had been torn down during the torrential rains. To find the missing mules, Cody said he and Pete would head through the narrow path on the McKay place and then north on Jones Creek Road—the rougher part of the path. Chet would head south on the section that was traveled more since there were two or three cabins closer to Morse Mill and the road that was named after it.

After prodding Red up the steep grade, Chet reined in the horse and reached for his canteen for a drink. Even though there had been a heavy rain the night before, the bright sun was doing its job to heat up the countryside. Steam was coming up from the wet ground. Chet thought the temperature might be close to eighty degrees and it hadn't even reached mid-morning.

"Well Red, with all of this rain there should be a big pool of water on Jones Creek where we can get you a drink. And if we're lucky, we'll find those missing mules wettin' their whistles as well."

Once he reached the rise in the road Chet spotted the big bluff that hid one of the largest pools of water along the creek. It was a popular place for youngsters to swim after a heavy rain. Once around it, Red could get a drink—and just maybe, Chet would find the long-eared equines.

When Red reached the pool Chet spotted an animal, but it wasn't a mule and it wasn't loose. It was a white Arabian, probably the only one in the state of Missouri. It had a distinctive short back, and to Chet's way of thinking, a "funny-looking head" compared to any other horse he'd seen in his lifetime. The horse was wearing an English saddle and a bridle with rhinestones attached to the brow band, noseband and cheek strap—and then there were those spur scars on its flanks.

Chet knew the horse at first glance, just like everybody else who lived in Jefferson County. Orville Simpson had brought it back from the Chicago World's Fair, also known as the 1893 World's Columbian Exposition. Newspapers from Chicago to St. Louis, and even Kansas City, wrote about it. The owner of the Arabian horses at the show had gone belly-up when funding failed to arrive as planned. Simpson, as always, bought the horse for pennies on the dollar and gave it to his daughter. A lot of ranchers wanted to breed their studs with the filly but Lori had refused, saying she wanted the horse to be as pure as she was. That in itself seemed a little odd with Chet having personal knowledge of the girl's history.

The now ten-year-old mare was hobbled and eating grass. Beside it was a neatly folded set of clothes—a red vest, a cream-colored blouse, pure white riding jodhpurs, black English riding boots with spurs, socks, and undergarments.

Chet knew better than to go forward—but Red was thirsty. At least that's what he told himself as he nudged his mount onward. Once around the corner Red needed no coaxing to walk into the stream. He lowered his head and drank some of the fresh clear water.

Twenty feet away in the deep end of the pool was Lori Simpson. Only her head and bare shoulders were above the water.

"Well look who's come all this way just to see little old me," Lori said.

Chet squinted into the sun toward Lori and urged Red on farther into the water. After traveling nearly ten feet into the stream the water was only up to the horse's knees.

"It don't appear that it rained as hard as I thought it did," he said, noticing that his saddle stirrups were still above water.

Lori's golden blonde hair was hanging down over the front of her shoulders.

"It's not," she said, as she used both hands to push back her hair. She had been kneeling in the pool, but decided to stand once she saw her former lover. "It's not deep at all," she said. "You should come in and join me. I'd really like some company."

Chet continued to gaze at her as more of her china-white skin emerged from the water. The waterline didn't quite cover her thighs.

"Looks a little cold to me," Chet said with a slight grin on his face.

"Well, you don't have to come in if you don't want to," she purred. "Silly me, I forgot my towel. We could lay out on the grass together and 'talk' while I dry off in the sunshine!"

"Those days are over Lori," he said. "Callie and I are getting married in May. You take care. I've got some mules to find. That's the only reason I'm out here."

"That's not true," she said. "You knew I'd be out here, just like the good old days when we were together."

"So long," he said, tipping his Stetson.

"You're marrying that little red-headed bitch instead of me!"

Just then, on his own, Red moved forward a few feet. He stretched out his legs and lifted his tail. He then proceeded to deposit a bountiful amount of green-from-the-grass feces into the pool. As each dropping splashed into the water it began to dissolve and ripples of the contaminated water began to spread out into what had been clear. To make matters worse Red stretched even more and began to relieve his body of urine. As the dissolving feces and the yellow-colored fluid flowed closer and closer to where Lori stood, she jumped back.

"You bastard! You made him do that. You're passing this up for a Kansas City whore," she said, now with her hands on her waist. "You'll live to regret it."

As Lori continued to yell, she noticed a strange look on Chet's face. He squinted, looking looking into her eyes.

Maybe I've said too much, she thought to herself.

Chet pulled the Colt from his gun belt.

He pulled back the hammer. Lori was looking at the nose of the barrel as he squinted his eyes even more.

"No, don't! I didn't mean it. She's a nice girl, truly a nice girl!"

Chet squeezed the trigger.

Red skidded back several feet. His ears were straight back on his head.

Lori, now with her face beet red and her body shaking, turned to her side and saw what remained of a water moccasin snake floating next to her in the water. Some of the skin and flesh had splattered onto her stomach and right breast. She spit up, vomiting where she stood.

"You better get out of the water and get back home," Chet said. "Where there's one snake, there's usually at least one more."

Still shaking, Lori scampered toward dry land but slipped on the shore's brown slimy mud, falling flat on her stomach and chest. She crawled a few more feet through the sludge and got back on her feet and ran to her horse. With nothing to clean herself with, she turned her back to Chet and began putting her clothes on over her mud-covered torso.

Chet grabbed his hat by the front and rear of the brim and pulled it down tightly on his head. Then he carefully coaxed Red around the bluff, heading north on Jones Creek Road. He stopped for a minute, rolled a cigarette and lit it. Red's ears perked up at the sound of the match striking Chet's belt buckle.

"Well sport, I think we ought to keep this little episode to ourselves, don't you think?"

The horse flipped his ears forward. Chet urged him to move along.

Ten minutes up the road Chet spotted Cody and Pete, each leading two yearling bay mules.

"I heard a shot," Cody said. "Did you see a coyote?"

"Just a couple of snakes," Chet said. "Shot one, the other slithered away."

GROUNDED

Over the next several weeks Chet continued to work on getting his strength back. There were young horse colts from the Harbison farm and bull calves at the Cavanaugh place to castrate before they started feeling their oats like grown stallions and "real bulls." No one said much, but Chet could tell that Pops, Ma, Cody, Callie, and especially Lize, had been watching him like a hawk to make sure he didn't "overdo it." Although Chet felt like he had made a full recovery, Pops laid down the law when it was time to take a herd of horses and mules to a government sale.

"Chet, I know you're feeling better, but it just makes more sense for you to stay home and take care of the ranch," Pops said. "We've got ten head of mules and twenty head of green-broke Morgans to get to Cedar Hill by this afternoon for them Army bigwigs. You've already done your share by helping round them all up. Mother, Beth, Little Cody, and me will go in the buggy with the supplies and Pete has agreed to help Cody and George with the stock. You don't want to get all banged up just before the wedding. We're probably going to be herding some of Callie's calves up to St. Louis this summer. You can be in charge of that and even take Callie to the city for a short visit."

"Okay, but I don't like it. I feel like I'm not doing my share," Chet said.

"Watching over our farm and Callie's place is plenty for one man to do," Pops said. "With that big rain last night, you'd better be checking Callie's stock. I hadn't seen so much lightning and heard so much thunder in a long time. It would be best if you checked to see if you lost any calves in the storm. I once saw five head of steers fried by a strike of lightning as they were huddled under a tree."

Pops made a point of trying not to be pushy with his boys, but in this instance his word was final. Chet knew he was grounded.

The rain the night before had caused problems on streams and rivers throughout the county. The Big River in Cedar Hill was no different and Clarence Nickerson found himself in the middle of that pouring rain as he came close to reaching his destination from St. Louis.

"Dam it, if this was any shit of a town, there would be a bridge here!" The canopy was up on the buggy he had rented, but rain from the west pelted his face and the black derby hat that he wore was soaked and dripping from the brim onto the front of his coat. A farmer watching from the other side of the river noticed that the buggy seat the man sat in could easily carry two adults and maybe even a small child. But to say the traveler had a wide girth would be an understatement. Nickerson took up more than half the overstuffed leather upholstered seat. The buggy springs were so compressed that water from the river covered the floorboards—and his ankle-high laced dress shoes.

Although the horse was doing its best to wade through the current, it moved from right to left as the man continued to crack his whip at the horse's flanks. The farmer, feeling sorry for the animal, finally waded out to the horse and led it the short distance to the shore.

Without thanking the farmer for his help, Nickerson bellowed: "How damn far is it to the hotel in this God-forsaken town?"

"It's about a mile up the road, but you won't find any rooms there," the farmer replied.

"Why the hell not?" Nickerson asked.

"Simple," he said. "The Army is here buyin' horses and mules from all the local breeders. It's only got six rooms. The soldiers have most of them. The ranchers are staying with friends, and more will be comin' tomorrow. My house has guests all the way from St. Clair."

"It's just what you'd expect from a shit-hole place like this," Nickerson said. "I have to find a room."

"You might try Billy Joe's Roadhouse. It's two miles down on the right. You can't miss it. It's a long log cabin with ivy growing all over it. It's not much, but it's mostly dry."

Nickerson cracked the whip again, this time over the horse's head, and the animal responded by picking up its feet and splashing mud as it ambled up the road to the inn. The farmer stood in the rain watching, shaking his head.

Dripping wet, Nickerson waddled into the saloon and approached the innkeeper. "I need the finest room you have, sir."

Those standing alongside the rough wooden-plank bar in the smoke-filled room looked up and laughed at the city slicker's request. Nickerson turned red and it looked as if steam would soon be spouting from his ears.

The man behind the bar was Billy Joe Smith. At least that's what he called himself when he moved into Cedar Hill ten years ago. Nickerson, who was about normal height, had to look up to talk to the man with the thinning silver hair. Tobacco-juice stains marked the corners of the innkeeper's mouth. The soiled bib overalls, partially covered the faded red long johns underneath. The sleeves of his underwear had been torn off at the shoulders and Nickerson could tell Smith was a man of strength by size of his biceps.

The innkeeper had claimed to be a Union soldier during the War Between the States, but many in Cedar Hill believed he was a Kansas Jayhawker, who took advantage of the battles by pillaging innocent farm families while their menfolk were out fighting for the North or the South.

"I got two rooms and they're both fifty cents a night—a dollar if you want me to sprinkle some sulfur on the mattress so it's not so ticky, and another dollar if you want some company," Smith said

Billy Joe pointed to two women in the back corner of the bar dressed only in undergarments with their hands up to the lantern trying to stay warm. One looked to be about fifteen.

She was skinny as a rail and her mousy brown hair looked as if it had never seen a comb. The other was a buxom woman of about forty who was nearly as big as Nickerson. Her dark hair was curly and matted. She smiled at the portly man and showed that one of her front teeth was missing.

"I'll take the one on right, but powder the mattress first," Nickerson said.

"That's my little sis, Nell," Smith said. "She's a real friendly one."

Nickerson ordered whiskey and sat at a separate table as the woman in her bare feet took a can of dusting powder from behind the bar and walked down the hall to the first room. Moments later she poked her head out the door.

"I'm all ready, Sugar," she said, again showing the gap between her teeth.

Nickerson jumped from his seat and ambled down the hall where she waited.

A soldier sitting at the bar with a fellow Army friend turned to the other: "He'd be wise to sprinkle that powder all over that flab of hers so he don't catch the itches from that soiled dove."

Smith grabbed the man by the collar and pushed him off his stool onto the dirt floor. Then he laughed. "He'll need more powder than what's in that can for that!"

The next morning Nickerson squinted out the small window of the room to see the sun out in full force, behind him on the bed was the naked fat woman, spread out on her back, taking up more than half the bed and snoring louder than anyone he had ever heard. He put on his clothes and walked down the hall to the bar where Billy Joe stood behind the counter, as if he hadn't moved all night.

Nickerson reached for the pot of coffee brewing on the stove in the center of the bar, scorched his hand on the hot handle, and dropped it back down. Billy Joe said nothing, but the smirk on his face couldn't be ignored. Nickerson used his handkerchief on the second attempt and filled one of the stained cups at the nearby table with the steaming-hot black coffee.

"What the hell is that fat bitch still doing in my room? Doesn't she even know she's supposed to leave after she's been poked? She woke me up this morning with her snoring."

Billy Joe took another puff of the fat cigar he had in his mouth. "Most men around here have the energy to poke her more than once," he said with a grin. "Besides, it's her room."

Nickerson made no reply, put his derby on his head and walked out the door and onto the muddy street. *Now if I can get that hick at the stable to get that damn horse hitched up to the buggy before the day's half over.*

Thirty minutes later Nickerson reined in the rental horse as he arrived at a small tarpaper shack sitting on stilts on the banks of the Big River. With a rumpled newspaper in one hand he pushed the door open with the other. Inside he found a ramshackle mess. Dirty pots and pans were scattered about and three men and one teenager were asleep on soiled cots. An empty stoneware jug that had held moonshine the night before was tipped over on the floor near Dutch Spragg's cot.

"Wake up, you worthless slug! You've done a half-assed job and you'd better make it right or we'll all be up in Jefferson City on death row."

Dutch Spragg staggered from the cot to a dirty washbowl and splashed water on his face. The remaining three brothers were awake as well, rubbing their eyes and wondering what the ruckus was about.

"Lester! Get the hell up and run down to the Pickett place," Dutch ordered. "See if you can fetch a slab of bacon out of their smokehouse without getting' peppered with rock salt." The skinny youth grabbed his hat off of a peg and walked out the door without bothering to put shoes on.

Nickerson grabbed at the only chair in the shack and eased himself into the seat, hoping it would not collapse under his weight.

"You jackass," he said. "You said there was no one else in the Cavanaugh house after you killed those three and set it on fire. This St. Louis newspaper says that bastard's daughter escaped the fire and now's living with a family named Harbison down the road. If she heard anything, the law is probably looking for us already. You've been paid three hundred dollars for an unfinished job. That little bitch has to die or we're sunk. If she's living with a whole damn family, how the hell are you going to kill her and keep us out of prison?"

Dutch Spragg's eyes lit up like a firecracker. "She ain't goin' ta be with hardly anyone this afternoon," he said. "Vince down at the stable said he had to make room in his

pasture for nearly thirty Harbison horses that were comin'
today. The whole family was a comin' except for that nigger
of theirs and that son of a bitch Rough Rider who jumped me
up in Grubville and stole my deer. They didn't mention no
other girl comin' with 'em, so she'll be there too."

Albert and Luke looked at each other at the same time
when Dutch mentioned the word "jumped" and "my deer."
They had been the ones ordered to haul the animal out of the
ravine. They had struggled to get the carcass on the back of
Luke's mule, and the two had to ride double on Albert's nag
when they brought it into the town in order for Dutch to take
the twenty-dollar prize.

"It's goin' be fun killin' Harbison and that nigger gal,"
Dutch said. "Hell you boys can even have a little fun with that
old woman like we did with that little girl that we found lost
in the woods a couple a years ago. You can keep it up well
after we shoot Harbison's brain's out. I got dibs on that girl
you're talkin' about Clarence. And I won't charge you an
extra dime. It will be my pleasure."

I don't care what you do," Nickerson said. "But we've got
to get it done and we can't let anyone see us."

"Nobody's goin' see us," Dutch said. "I know all the back
roads. Besides, anyone with any horses to sell is goin' to be
here today, not that hellhole Grubville. Can you ride a saddle
horse? A buggy won't make it through the way we're takin.'"

"If I must," Nickerson said. "Whatever it takes."

THE RECKONING

Cassie and Lize were waiting at noon when Chet and Red returned from the Cavanaugh place. Sweat was dripping from Chet's brow and Red had a light lather on his chest, but nothing like he did at the finish of his run to Mr. Lee's place months earlier.

"All your cows and calves seem to be doing okay," Chet said to his future bride. Last night's storm had 'em all under the trees, but Red and I, with the help of Pebbles, moved 'em all back out in the pasture where I could get a good count. You got some good timber up there that you should think about harvesting. That would give you more pasture and you could build the herd back up to about forty-five head or so. It would give us plenty of lumber for a solid house."

"It's not just my farm; it's yours too," she said. "Do we have to cut down all the trees? They're so pretty."

"Only about ten percent," he said. "That'll give us about thirty more acres of pasture without harming the watershed. If we stripped the entire woods a big rain like last night's could cause the creeks to overflow somethin' terrible. It'd flood the stud barn and maybe even Ma and Pops' house."

Chet slid out of the saddle, unknotted the cinch and tossed the saddle up on the top of the split-rail fence. He grabbed the saddle blanket and rubbed the sweat off the gelding.

"I sure hope you two have something good for dinner," he said. "I'm so hungry I could eat a horse."

Lize couldn't help but bellow out a bawdy-sounding laugh.

"That-there horse of yours is givin' you a funny look," she said. "It's a darn good thing that gal of yours and me got a beef roast ready to pull outta the oven."

Chet placed a rope halter around Red's head and led him back to his stall where some fresh oats were waiting. Chet turned his head back to Callie and Lize. "I'll be back to inspect all that good cookin' as soon as I get Red taken care of."

On his arrival to the kitchen, Callie was busy slicing fresh bread and Lize was adding flour to the drippings for gravy. Mashed potatoes were waiting and green beans that had been canned last fall were heating on the stove.

Chet pumped fresh water into the washbowl at the sink and then walked it over to the small table by the kitchen window where he splashed water onto his face and began to clean himself up. As he was finishing drying his face, he looked up and out the window after hearing a very unfamiliar sound.

"What in God's name is that fool dog barking about?" Lize asked as she placed the plates on the kitchen table.

"Pebbles don't bark at anything," Chet said as he looked out the window once more. A second later, a shot rang out shattering the pane of glass with shards of glass slicing into Chet's forehead.

"Get down! Get down!"

Lize pushed Callie to the floor, covering her with her own body.

Chet leaped for the pantry door and grabbed his rifle, along with a box of special-order cartridges. He wiped the blood that was running over his eyes and peered out the window. He saw black-powder smoke coming from the open hayloft. What he couldn't see from his angle was Albert Spragg holding a Winchester lever action with both hands and his right leg braced against the loft-door frame. Chet fired four rapid shots into the opening, shattering hardened oak wood all around the second oldest of the Spragg brothers. The fourth shot struck so close to Albert's foot that he jerked back his leg losing his balance.

Chet had moved his head to the side of the window to avoid another shot aimed at him from the creek bed but he heard the man's scream of agony as Albert hit the muddy ground below the barn loft. The rifle was still in the loft and Albert let everyone know it.

"Dutch help me! I'm hurt bad. I don't got a gun no more and a bone's pokin' out the side of my leg!"

"Just shut up until we're finished here," was Dutch's only reply. He then directed his shout toward the white clapboard farmhouse.

"This is goin' cost you even more now Harbison," he said as he signaled Luke. Again it was another gunshot, but this one was muffled coming from one of the barn stalls inside. Samson shouted out a pain-stricken bray that continued but became weaker and weaker by the second until the jack was silent.

"That's one Harbison ass gone and you're next," Dutch shouted. "And it's goin' ta be slow and painful. You'll get to listen to us as we take turns with that nigger of yours, and me with that Cavanaugh gal. Then we're goin' burn the whole place down, just like we did up the road.

"We've got to get outta here fast!" Chet ordered as he filled his pockets with cartridges and reached for his Colt.

Callie managed to get out from under Lize. The young woman had tears in her eyes when she looked up from Lize toward Chet. The former slave wouldn't be leaving with them. Callie was soaked with blood and there was a bullet hole in Lize's chest. There were no last words from the woman who had spent more than sixty years at the Harbison farm.

"Give it up Harbison!" Nickerson shouted. "You've got no place to go. We won't burn the house if you come out now. That'll leave something for your kinfolk."

"That voice, I heard that voice the night they killed Mother and Father," Callie said. "I thought I was dreaming, but I heard that exact voice!"

"We've got to go now and there's only one way out," Chet said. He grabbed Callie by the arm almost dragging her to the hallway near her bedroom.

Blood was still flowing from Chet's forehead and blinding his eyes. Callie ripped a section of her cotton apron and wrapped it around Chet's head to slow down the flow of blood.

Dropping to his knees, Chet grabbed the hand-made rag rug from the floor and tossed it to the side. Then he placed two of his fingers in the small holes drilled into the floorboards and lifted a two-foot by three-foot section of flooring. All the while he could hear the spray of bullets shattering the kitchen and dining room windows just a few feet away.

"Grandpa dug this out during the Civil War so his family could escape bushwhackers," Chet said. "Cody and I used to play down here when Pops and Ma were away. It hasn't been used in years."

Trying not to be rough, he lowered Callie down into the opening that was filled with cobwebs. Although there was about twelve to fourteen inches of space where a stone foundation had been built below the floorboards, Grandpa had dug a trench two feet deeper heading in a westerly path.

"Keep following the tunnel," he said. "It will lead to underneath the front porch. From there we can crawl to the ditch. If they're all down near the creek they won't see us behind the hedge in the yard."

Callie followed Chet's orders and within less than a few minutes she was pushing away a rotted board that led to underneath the front porch. Chet turned his rifle around and rammed the butt of it through the wooden latticework that surrounded the space under the porch.

"We need to stay low and run to the ditch as fast as we can," he said. There was no hesitation as the two bent down as low as possible and sprinted to and dived into the ditch. Chet poked his head up for a split second, spying Dutch, Luke and a fat man in a suit all firing into the house. Albert continued to beg for help as he lay in the mud in agonizing pain, but was ignored by all three of his cohorts.

Chet pulled the revolver from his belt and handed it to Callie.

"Remember what I showed you," he said. "If anyone gets near you, pull the hammer back and squeeze the trigger. You have five shots to get them. But that's not likely to happen. I'm going to put all three of them into a run."

Chet, covered in blood, mud, and cobwebs, grabbed the Krag-Jorgensen and crawled toward where the ditch drained into the creek. Once there he took a careful look and sprang to his feet firing another four rounds one after another at the remaining three enemies. It was like he was back in Cuba, but this time he was more prepared.

One bullet caught Dutch in his right calf. The oldest of the Spraggs whirled around like lightning and fired off three shots from a revolver—all three flying over Chet's head as he hunkered back down in the mud.

"Where the hell is that bastard?" Dutch shouted. "I can't see 'im or any rifle smoke!"

Nickerson darted back toward the Cavanaugh place, splashing through the creek and tugging on the reins as he tried to get his horse to follow him to the main gate that exited the farm. His face was red and his breathing was heavy. He no longer wanted to be part of the battle.

By now Chet had reloaded the rifle and fired three more shots at the remaining two men hovering behind the trunk of the large sycamore tree. Blood stung Chet's eyes but he knew his aim was close.

Luke's mule jerked hard with the reins burning his palms as they pulled through his hand. It ran off, following Dutch's pinto, now in a dead run up the hill.

Dutch, dragging his right leg ran east down the creek bed with the red barn in his sights. Luke ran in the same direction but darted right, heading toward the springhouse.

Chet dropped three more cartridges inside the rifle's magazine, pointing and firing at Dutch. With blood seeping through his bandages and down his face Chet's vision began to blur even more. All five shots were close, but they hit the muddy pasture behind the man dragging his one leg. But there was a silver lining. Dutch had returned fire two more times. The revolver was likely empty and Dutch wasn't wearing a gun belt for extra ammo.

By now, Chet had reloaded the rifle one more time, with the last three cartridges from his pockets. Dutch continued his escape with his only chance being able to catch Ashes or Buck; both in the paddock in front the barn.

That wasn't going to happen.

Chet fired two rounds, aiming just shy of the horses, spooking them enough where they reared as Dutch tried to reach for the dapple grey mare. Both horses ran off.

He fired his last round at Dutch as the man slammed his body through the barn door.

"I'm not through with you or that hunk-of-shit horse of yours Harbison!" Dutch shouted from inside the barn as he squeezed the trigger once more. Chet felt a burning sting to the top of his left shoulder. The bullet had ripped through a layer of flesh, but hadn't hit any bones. If it had been a few inches in the other direction it would have ripped through his neck.

With no cartridges left, Chet found himself taking shelter behind the stone chimney of the old slave cabin but he pointed the rifle toward the springhouse. There was no place left for Luke to go.

"Don't shoot! Don't shoot!" Luke shouted. "I've been bit by a copperhead. I give up. I need a doctor. I don't want to die! Pointing his empty rifle at Luke, Chet told him to come his way and throw his revolver towards him. Luke obeyed without questioning. Still acting like the rifle was loaded, Chet walked up to where the Remington laid and retrieved it.

As Chet faced Luke down he heard the muffled sound of a revolver firing inside the barn, along with barking and a deep growling of Pebbles. Then it was silent.

"You ain't goin' die, not if you listen to me, Luke," Chet said. "Don't move an inch. If you do, that poison will spread through your body like wildfire and you'll be dead in five minutes." It was a bluff, but it worked. Luke stayed still and said he would wait until help arrived.

Now with a loaded handgun Chet stepped lightly to the red barn, staying far to the west of the building, he ran from tree to tree. *Damn, I thought he was out of cartridges*, Chet said to himself. As he got closer he again heard the low growling sound of the dog, but not a word from the mouth of Dutch Spragg. With the hammer back on the revolver, Chet entered the barn with his arms stretched out and ready to fire. But there would be no need for that.

He saw Pebbles, now at ease. The dog's muzzle was covered with blood. Red was backed up to the far side of his stall. The whites of the gelding's eyes showed more than his pupils. His ears, laid straight back. The gelding continued to be skittish even as he heard his owner's voice. Two feet away from the horse lay Dutch Spragg. Nearly the entire calf of his right leg had been gnawed away, leaving the straw on the stall floor soaked with blood. Taking a closer look Chet saw that Dutch's skull was crushed. Blood stained Red's front hooves.

Chet led Red out of the barn and into the paddock and Pebbles followed.

Now to get Cassie out of that ditch and get that other fella, whoever in hell he is, Chet thought. But Cassie wasn't where he had left her. Then he looked down the road near the gate.

The stranger was frantic, trying to open the gate, but had no idea how the pulley system worked. Callie was walking toward the stranger with both hands on the revolver. The barrel was pointed at the man's head.

Chet ran down the road as fast as he could with Pebbles at his heels.

"Cassie don't! Don't do it!"

He arrived in seconds, short on breath and unable to repeat his words. Blood from his shoulder wound had soaked the entire left side of his shirt. Cassie had the Colt's hammer pulled back and her right index finger on trigger. Nickerson stood still, his face drenched with sweat and his hands shaking as he held them up in the air.

"He's the one who had Mother, Father, and Agnus killed, all over some stupid land. Then he had them shoot Lize, too," she said. "He could have taken Father to court, but he had them all killed instead."

"Put the gun down, Cassie," Chet said, still breathing heavily. "He ain't worth the price of a bullet. Think how I was when I came back home. You don't want to go through that. You'll get justice. This hunk of horse shit is going to hang from a rope in Hillsboro."

She lowered the six-shooter and handed it to Chet. Nickerson gave a sigh of relief, lowered his hands and wiped the heavy sweat off his brow.

"I can make up for all of this," Nickerson said. "Just let me go and I can provide you with enough money where you will never have to work again," he begged.

"You'd better shut up, mister, or I'll give her back the gun," Chet said.

"Chet, you're hurt bad. She grabbed a hankie from her jean's pocket and reached into his shirt to cover the wound."

"It's not that bad, really," he said.

"Cassie, please go back to the paddock and catch one of the horses. Get Mr. Frost or Mr. Nelson to get down here as quick as you can." He looked at his shoulder, which was still bleeding. I guess you'd better have them call Doc Bockey too. I'm not the only one that's going to need tending to. Don't go in the house. We'll take care of that later."

Callie paused for a second, clutched Chet's left hand and kissed him on his cheek. She used her sleeve to wipe the blood from his eyes, then, she tore another piece of cloth off of her apron and tied it around his forehead. She turned and ran toward the barn. Pebbles followed her.

Chet pointed the Colt straight at Nickerson's head.

"Take off your hat and coat and empty out all your pockets," Chet said. "I don't want any surprises from you. I've shot my share of men in Cuba and I won't hesitate to pull the trigger on you—and no more talk of deals. It ain't gonna' happen.

Callie, breathing heavily, reached the paddock within a few minutes. Buck and Ashes were now on the far side of the pasture, nearly 500 yards away. She called their names but other than lifting their heads, they remained still. But there stood Red only a short distance from the barn. She reached for his bridle on the gatepost and then whistled.

"Come on boy, you've got to come to me."

The horse raised his head and his ears perked up. He eased toward the woman who had taken care of him while his master had been ill.

"Come on boy, all the way." The horse continued toward her with his head swaying back and forth. As he reached her, he lowered his head and allowed Callie to pet him and put his headstall on, just as he had done during their winter exercise sessions. Callie walked the horse out of the gate and positioned the tall steed along side of the fence railing.

"We can do this," she whispered. "We have to do this to help Chet."

Red stood as still as a statue, and with Callie still holding the reins, she climbed the fence to the second rail that allowed her to straddle the horse's back. To her surprise, Red extended out his four legs, lowering his back closer to the ground. She climbed on without incident. Holding his reins tight, she moved her hands down to his lower neck and grabbed onto a section of his mane as well.

"Come on boy, let's go."

With his neck bowed and his head down, Red pranced in short steps toward the entrance of the farm acting as if he was ready to run.

Chet pulled his pocket watch from his jeans to see how much time had passed, and then looked up at the prisoner before putting it back in his pocket. He rubbed his eyes as he saw the tall horse traveling in his direction.

"Damn! I don't believe it," he said.

196

"The other horses wouldn't come," Callie said, almost as if she was apologizing.

"Are you okay?" he asked.

"Red and I can handle this," she said, as she patted the horse's neck.

Chet walked over and pulled the rope that opened the gate.

"I love you," Chet said.

"I love you too," Callie said as she turned to Chet, and at the same time, she nudged the horse to encourage him through the opening. Once she cleared the gate she flipped the reins. Red took her cue and galloped off throwing mud clogs behind him.

Callie held her thighs and knees tight to the horse's body. She gave the reins more slack to allow the horse his head to run, but kept a tight hold the leather straps and his mane. As they reached the top of the hill near the end of the farm road Red picked up his pace. Callie pulled the reins along his neck a little too hard, and as the horse turned right toward town she started to slide off of his back. She grabbed higher up on the horse's neck, grabbed another clump of mane and pulled herself back into position. Red was now in a full gallop and Callie wondered if she would ever be able to stop him.

As the tavern and general store came into sight she leaned back and took up the slack in the reins. Red began to slow down as he bowed his head and started his walking prance.

No one was outside and Callie couldn't risk climbing down. "Mr. Frost, Mr. Nelson, Chet's hurt and needs help!"

Both men ran out the front door of the tavern.

"It's the Spraggs," she said. "They've killed Lize and shot Chet. Call the doctor! Nelson ran back inside to make the phone call while Wheeler grabbed his .12-gauge pump and a .16-gauge double barrel from behind the bar.

Callie spun Red around on his hind legs and took off back to the farm. Wheeler and Nelson jumped into the spring wagon and followed, amazed that the girl was riding a horse that everyone believed only Chet could handle.

Callie had a hard time keeping her balance once she reached the farm road, but managed to stay atop the horse grasping the reins and his mane at the same time. Red's speed did not faulter.

Chet was sitting on a stump, still pointing the revolver at Nickerson, with Pebbles at his side, growling every time the prisoner tried to move. Then he heard the sound of hoof beats. Callie was still holding her own when the sorrel horse came to an abrupt stop along side the gate. Chet smiled a smile of relief, and disbelief, as she slid down from the horse but she stumbled a little and had to grab the fence railing with both hands.

"He did it, he did everything I wanted him to," Callie said. "He was amazing. Mr. Frost and Mr. Nelson are coming. They're right behind me."

"He's not the only one that's amazing," he said. "You've got the touch. I didn't think he'd ever let anyone ride him except me. You're amazing in more ways than one."

Within minutes, Wheeler Frost and Nelson could be seen in a buckboard coming down the road. There was no holding back on the reins. Wheeler's horse was in a full gallop and Nelson held two shotguns in his arms while still managing to stay in his seat. Moments later, the two were followed by Cohen Lee in his mail wagon. He had seen the buckboard turn down Harbison Road at breakneck speed and knew he had to follow suit.

By now Callie was kneeling next to Chet, putting pressure on his shoulder wound. She wiped the tears from her face as Chet did his best to explain to the three men what had just taken place. As Wheeler listened, Cohen Lee tied Nickerson's hands behind his back with a piece of rope from his wagon. Almost as nervous as Nickerson, Nelson kept his shotgun pointed at the city slicker. The storekeeper's stance was as stiff as any soldier's and his finger stayed on the trigger.

"Chet, you take Callie back to my place in the mail wagon," Mr. Lee said. "We can even tie Red to the back of the wagon for you. Marcella will be there to help patch you up and calm both of you down until the doctor gets there; we'll watch for him. Wheeler, Nelson, and I will take care of Lize. We'll keep her in Wheeler's ice house, until the proper time."

"We'll lock this bastard and the Spragg boys down in my cellar until the sheriff can come for them," Wheeler said. "I'll drag Dutch behind the chicken house until the deputies can haul him off."

"Chet, don't worry about the house," Nelson said. "Me and the Missus will clean it up and I'll get help to fix up the windows. You do what Mr. Lee says. We'll take care of all of this."

PUTTING THE PUZZLE TOGETHER

Two days passed. A small funeral was held for Lize and she was buried in the Harbison cemetery in the corner the north forty pasture. It was a small gathering—the new preacher, the Harbison family, Callie, Cohen and Marcella Lee, Wheeler Frost, Nelson and his wife, George Timmons, and Pete McKinney.

Pops said the last words. "Lize had a rough start in life, but all of us tried to make her feel that this was her home," he said. "We tried, but we may have failed in some ways. At least she is at peace with the Lord."

They returned to the farmhouse where Helen, Beth and Callie had prepared a meal for those who had attended the ceremony.

"I sure am goin' miss her hollering at me for not wipin' my feet, asking for seconds, and cussin'," Pete said.

"Yeah, she sure got a kick outta doin' that to you,' George said with a grin. "I'm gonna miss her a heap, too."

"She took care of all of us when we were kids," Chet said. "Like we were hers."

When they finished their meals and stories, Cody was the first to get up. He hadn't touched much on his plate. "George, could you help me out by the blacksmith shed? There's somethin' we gotta do."

As the two left the kitchen, Mr. Lee stood up. "I know that there's never goin' to be a good time for this, but it has to be said. I've been visiting with the sheriff. Federal Marshals are comin' down from Kansas City to investigate this case. There's not a lot of good news, 'cept that Nickerson, along with Albert and Luke Spragg, have all been charged with murder and there ain't a jury around that won't give them the noose after they hear what went on. They're all locked up tight at the county jail in Hillsboro. Like Nickerson told Callie, the whole thing had to do with a land deal out West that Mr. Cavanaugh and some other fella put together, and Nickerson came out on the short end of the deal.

"That Colt Bisley revolver that Chet got from Dutch after the shootin' spree? Well, Wheeler will tell you it's the same one he sold to Callie's father after Chet and Pete here caused all that commotion about that three-toed mountain lion returnin' to the county. They must have taken it from Mr. Cavanaugh during that encounter before the fire. All of 'em are tryin' to cover their tracks. Nickerson is tellin' the sheriff that he just took the Spragg boys to rough up Cavanaugh to find out where all the money was, and they got out of hand and killed him. The Spraggs are both sayin' that it was Nickerson who did all the dirty work. They were there as his body guards and then things got out of hand with Nickerson shootin' everyone after he lost his temper. I don't think anything they say will be believed by a jury, and like I said, the marshals are goin' be down here with more investigatin' to do."

The family members and their guests continued to talk about Lize again and all their memories, most of them humorous.

Beth wondered what was going on with her husband and walked to the blacksmith shed to see. George stopped her before she reached the shed door.

"I wouldn't go in there Miz Beth, George said. "Cody probably don't want to have a woman—especially you—see him cryin' like he is."

"What is it?" she asked. "He's been awful quiet like ever since we got back from Cedar Hill.

George looked down at his boots and started to shuffle. "After Mr. Frost got on the phone to tell you folks what happened, you and Little Cody, and Mr. and Mrs. Harbison loaded up the buggy and headed back home. Cody had us go with him to the stonecutter in Cedar Hill to get a grave marker for Miz Lize. Word had spread like wildfire about the shootin' since everyone knew the Spraggs.

"Cody had the proper words all written on a piece of paper and the man refused to do the work. Said it was against the law in Missouri to put a nigger's name—that's what he said, not me—on a marker. Cody was holdin' his temper back and then asked the fella to sell him a headstone. He refused that too 'cause he didn't want to be involved in sellin' one for a uh, uh, colored woman. I thought Cody was goin' tear that man's head off. It took all we had for me and Pete to hold him back and so he wouldn't beat the stuffin's outta that peckerwood.

"Cody found a big flat stone down in the creek this morning," George said. "Nothin's too big for him to lift, but this one was wider than his arms all stretched out. I helped him carry it into the shed so he could trim it down and put words on it."

Beth walked up to the shed window and wiped some of the dirt away with her handkerchief. Inside she saw her husband with a chisel and small hammer. He had almost finished the stone. In crudely cut letters it read: "Lize Wilson, a Member of the Harbison Family."

"Come on George," she said. "Let's go back in the house. Momma Helen has peach pie you and I should get into."

"Uh, I can't," he said. I gotta git down to Luebbering to help Anna, uh I mean Miss Anna Rose. That farm of hers has what she calls 'potential' but it needs a lot of work to make it right. It's been that way long before her husband died."

"Do you want to take a piece of pie with you?"

"No, she promised to make supper for us and her pa," George said. "She's got a real good knack of makin' a powerful good supper."

As the days passed, Callie, Beth and Helen continued to sew the wedding dress, along with the one Beth would wear as matron of honor. All three continued to look out the balcony window of Beth and Cody's room from time to time as more men were seen in the distance. Some were searching through the remains of the Cavanaugh farmhouse rubble while others searched the barn. They could see men with pitchforks emptying the loft of its hay.

"I sure don't think there's anything to be found," Beth said. Cody and Pops sifted through the house after the heavy rain and there just wasn't anything left. They could hardly make out the…"

And then she stopped.

"It's okay Beth," Callie said. "I know. They couldn't hardly make out the bodies of Mother, Father, or Agnus. It's okay. I miss them terribly, but you're my new family. I don't know what I would have done without you. I think of you as my big sister now. And without you, Chet and I may have never gotten to know each other."

The noon hour neared and the women returned to the kitchen to fix sandwiches for the men. A ham from the smokehouse, fresh bread and even leaf lettuce from the garden would make for a good meal in the summer-like weather.

As the men and the women gathered in the kitchen, they spotted a familiar sight coming down the road. It was Dolly, pulling the mail wagon, with Mr. Lee allowing the horse to travel at a faster clip than normal.

"You're just in time for dinner," Helen said, as she opened the screen door for him.

"I've got more news from the Sheriff Calvert and one of the marshals," Cohen said as he climbed down from the wagon. "Callie and you folks will be getting a letter from the government soon, but it won't have all the details that I got up at Wheeler's talkin' to them earlier today.

"They've started to put the pieces of the puzzle together. Callie, I'm just repeating what they told me so please don't think poorly of me, please."

"I understand," Callie said.

"As you know, your pa was a businessman, buyin' and sellin' property and such. Well just before you moved here, he hit rock bottom. There were some bad investments and some of the folks he dealt with hit rock bottom as well. To put it plainly, your pa went broke. The lenders were about to foreclose on that red brick house you had in Kansas City, and your pa was desperate.

"He got approached by a fella by the name of Bigalow. This fella had sold lots of stock and bonds and had a reputation that some folks didn't like. He was a harelip and couldn't talk good, but he could wheel and deal. He showed Mr. Cavanaugh some geological papers that showed where vast amounts of coal were in Colorado, and that the deposits were close to a rail line. Bigalow said he'd put up the seed money for your pa to buy the land. Then, they could make a steal and sell it to the mining companies."

"Well, it worked," Cohen said. "They bought the land for pennies and sold it for dollars. They each made a fortune. Bigalow took his money and ran. They think he's somewhere in Argentina.

"Whether your pa knew it was a scam in the beginning— well, we'll never know, but the marshals did find the original geological report in the bottom of a tool chest in the barn. It was under a fake bottom."

"I bet that's why he wouldn't let Pete open it to look for a pair of gloves," Chet said.

"More than twenty coal company shareholders lost their shirts in the deal with the biggest one being Nickerson. He bought more than half the land with his own money, and encouraged his friends to buy the rest. It turns out the geological papers were forgeries. Nickerson hired a retired Pinkerton agent to track down your pa and his partner."

"Instead of changing his name where you and your mother would ask questions, your father moved to this little old town, probably because he figured no one could track him here if he laid low. But that Pinkerton man was a persistent cuss. He bribed a teller at the First Bank of Kansas City, who had mailed a bank draft from there down here to Grubville. That's when Nickerson decided to hire the Spraggs to help him get what money he could back from your father."

"But if he knew all of this, why didn't Nickerson go to the law and have father arrested?" Callie asked.

"That's where it gets interesting, and it's not good news for you and Chet," Mr. Lee said.

"When the land deal turned out to be a scam, all the new landowners filed a federal lawsuit against Bigalow and Mr. Cavanaugh. The court ruled in the landowners' favor since Bigalow and your pa were in what they call 'absentia' and these landowners were to get all the money back, if they could find it. With Bigalow nowhere to be found, Nickerson knew he would be lucky to get fifty cents on the dollar if he turned Mr. Cavanaugh in, but if he could beat it out of him—sorry Callie—and he could get most of his money back, no one would be the wiser because your father wouldn't risk being arrested by reporting Nickerson. But something happened up at your house that went awry. Your family got killed, Nickerson didn't find any money and then he believed you witnessed the killing and had to put an end to you. He and the Spraggs weren't figuring on Chet and you getting the upper hand.

"And now for the disturbing part, the government couldn't find any of your pa's money either, except for a couple thousand dollars in the bank at St. Clair. That notice that you're going to be getting is for an auction of your farm. They're going to sell the whole thing off May 14, lock, stock, and barrel, including the cattle, the Standardbreds, the buggy, and even what money you earned from sellin' those cows last fall.

"Bigalow and your father made almost a hundred and twenty-five thousand dollars between the two of them, but no one knows where it went. So those folks in Colorado are going to get the five thousand or so that the farm and the livestock go for.

"I'm sorry, but you had to know," Mr. Lee said.

Callie squeezed Chet's hand. "That's just a week before our wedding. Maybe we need to postpone it."

"No matter what, we're getting married on May twenty-first," Chet said. "I've rented that empty cabin down the road for us and there's still plenty of work for me here where I can earn enough to buy a smaller spread. And I can even pick up some extra work if need-be."

"I've got an idea on how this might work for you two, but I have to finish my route," Mr. Lee said. "We'll get back together tomorrow with my idea."

As Mr. Lee walked out to the back porch, Pebbles jumped up and placed his front paws on Mr. Lee's waist to greet him.

"Chet, it sure was a good thing that your ma had a smart dog like this and you had that tall horse of yours. Who would have thought that an ol' dog dumped out on a country road to fend for himself and a skinny ol' horse that was nearly beaten to death would end up getting some revenge on one of the dregs of humanity—and then save the lives of a young couple ta' boot.

"I had a dog that was just a hair smarter than Pebbles here. But he had a dull spot when it came to playin' checkers. I could—"

"You could beat him two out of three tries," Callie said finishing his sentence. "I think just about everybody has heard that one by now!"

"Well I guess they have," Mr. Lee said with a smile.

"Let's all plan on meetin' at Wheeler's tomorrow after supper," Mr. Lee said. "It's Sunday and we can have the bar room all to ourselves. Chet, you might want to ask Pete and George to come by as well."

THE PLAN

Helen and Callie weren't accustomed to being inside Wheeler's feed store and bar, but Beth had told the two that she had been in there "once or twice" with Cody and there wasn't anything to worry themselves about.

By seven that evening, all who had been invited were in attendance and Wheeler provided sarsaparilla for everyone.

"I've had a chance to talk to about everyone on the mail route and then even passed the word along through Dr. Bockelman so he could have a say while making his rounds," Mr. Lee said.

"The farm and everything that goes with it is easily worth five thousand dollars, but with such short notice of the auction to outsiders, I think Chet, with the help from his pa and Cody, can get it for three thousand," Mr. Lee said. "Anyone who is a friend of the Harbisons or myself have agreed to come and bid, but will bow out when Chet gets close to the limit. That way it will look legitimate and the courts can't question it."

"What about Mr. Simpson? George asked. "He's always lookin' for somethin' for nothing."

"It's just a chance we'll have to take," Mr. Lee said. "He's never been much on cattle and he don't know a lick about plantin' anything."

"Yeah, and he's likely to back off as the price gets higher," Cody added.

"We've got nothing to lose," Chet said. "With me bein' a veteran, the bank might even loan me a couple hundred dollars to add to the pot. Heck, if we get in a bind and don't get the place, the way Red's been getting' along with Callie, we might just have to enter him in the county fair race with Callie on his back. Me and Pete can get up in the stands sayin' that we're bettin' on that freckle-faced gal on that funny long-legged horse. We could win enough for another smaller spread."

Callie made a fist and threw a light bunch into Chet's good shoulder and everyone at the table broke out in laughter. Deep inside, they knew the purchase of the Cavanaugh place was a longshot, even a longer shot than Callie taking Red to the Fourth of July race in Hillsboro.

AUCTION TIME

As the days passed the Harbisons did their best to sell off more of their yearlings and now had close to three thousand dollars in cash. There was no talk of replacing Samson in the near future. Buying the Cavanaugh farm was an urgent matter, both Pops and Helen agreed. Chet had obtained a loan for $500 from the bank because of his veterans' status and his family's good name. George and Pete each contributed $25 as an early wedding present.

"You'd might as well take it," Pete said when Chet tried to turn it down. "I'll just lose it in a poker game up in Cedar Hill if I keep it."

"Mr. Frost agreed that I should give this to ya'," George said. "He called it a good investment."

Chet and Callie would know their fate soon. The auction was only a few hours away.

By 10 a.m. more than a hundred people had arrived at the Cavanaugh place and had signed up to get their official auction numbers. Pops, Chet, Cody, George, and Pete joined the crowd and soon found themselves talking with Mr. Lee and Mr. Frost.

Helen Harbison had set up a table outside of the barn selling slices of pie and lemonade to those who came to the auction. It was bound to be a hot day.

"Callie, Beth and Little Cody ought to be here soon with some cake to sell as well," Helen told her friend, Mrs. Hoffman. "I hope Callie and Chet don't have their hopes set too high. Who knows what will happen at this auction with all these folks here. There are a lot of them I don't recognize."

Finally, at 11 a.m. a tall, dark-haired man wearing the biggest cowboy hat Helen had ever laid eyes on, stood up on the back of a wagon and explained the auction process.

"Hello folks, we've got a one-bid-takes-it-all sale here today," he said. "One hundred and seventy-five acres of pastureland and woods filled with red oak and sycamore trees, thirty-five head of registered Aberdeen Angus breeding stock, including one of the most powerful-looking seed bulls I've ever seen. All the cows will be dropping calves soon. Although there's no home, there's plenty of lumber out here to build a fine house, and we've got a barn that will hold plenty of hay and horses to boot."

As Helen waited for "the girls" to arrive she grimaced at the site of Orville Simpson being dropped off at the gates of the Cavanaugh entrance. Lori Simpson took the reins of the buggy from her father and continued down the road toward the Harbison farm. She was followed by a Simpson lumber wagon driven by Herb Smith. Smith had worked at the mill for fifteen years. Three of his fingers were missing on his right hand—a result of being continually told to speed up his work—he held the reins to his team very tightly with his left.

Helen looked further down the road where she saw Callie, Beth, and Little Cody in Pops' hunting wagon. The Simpson buggy as well and the Harbison wagon would reach the entrance gate to the Harbisons' at about the same time.

Oh, please dear Lord, don't let Beth kill that Simpson girl, Helen prayed. Please let her settle for a couple of slaps on that little brat's face.

As the two teams met, Beth pulled in the reins on Prince and stared Lori Simpson straight in the eyes.

"You'd better stop and turn that rig of yours around, girl. You're not allowed on Harbison land."

Callie remained silent as she held little Cody on her lap.

"Oh, I don't have any plans on comin' in," Lori said. "But if you three stay here much longer you won't be able to come out. My daddy is up there on the hill bidding on that crook's place right now. As soon as that auctioneer slams that gavel down that farm and the easement to this road will be ours. Mr. Smith here has orders to get that barbed wire out and string it across your entrance."

"The only crook around here is your pa," Beth said.

"You can't do that," Callie said as she handed Little Cody to Beth. "That's the only way out of this farm. The Harbisons have been using this road for decades."

"Well, our attorney has told us different," Lori said. "You'll have to exit from Jones Creek Road from now on. Besides Daddy's going to have this road blocked with all sorts of traffic. He's going to have to buy extra wagons to haul all the timber off of it to his mill. I'm so glad I begged Daddy to buy it. He'll triple his money and then he can sell whatever's left of it once the trees are cleared. That's what

Daddy does when someone breaks his little girl's heart," she said.

Callie jumped from the wagon and walked over to Lori.

"That dog don't hunt!" Callie said.

Beth's mouth hung wide open. That was one of Mr. Lee's favorite sayings and Beth was proud of the city girl's appreciation of it.

"Everyone knows you're the town tart," Callie said without hesitating. "You left Chet all by his lonesome. It wasn't the other way around. You ran off with that pots-and-pans peddler, except he dumped you after he got enough of what he wanted—and it wasn't just your smiling face and cheerful personality he was after. Then you tried to save face back here with your dear daddy by trying to snag Chet again. It's not going to happen girl!

"Until that gavel drops, this land still belongs to me and you're trespassing," Callie said. "And if you're not off of it in the next minute I'm goin' drag you down from your seat and tear into you like a wildcat—and everyone up on that hill, including that tightwad father of yours is going to hear and see it happen."

Callie's face was so red with rage that Beth couldn't see the freckles on the girl's cheeks. Beth and Little Cody watched as Lori frantically backed up the chestnut mare that was pulling her buggy. Once backed up to the gully, she pulled the reins in the opposite direction and then flipped them as hard as she could. The frantic horse took off leaving a cloud of dust, spraying dirt and sand as it raced off.

"I'll probably lose my job over this for not buttin' in," Herb said as he sat in the seat of the lumber wagon, holding his side. "But it'll be worth it after seein' the look on that brat's face when you told her what-fer Miss Callie."

"You done good girl," Beth said. "You had her bluff but good."

"What makes you think I was bluffing?" Callie said as she winked.

By now the auction was well underway. As Beth, Little Cody, and Callie made their way to the pie stand, Chet was making a bid of twenty-five hundred dollars. Neighbors had bowed out of the bidding by now but Orville Simpson remained a contender. "Twenty-six hundred," he shouted as he raised his number printed on a piece of card stock.

Callie walked up to and grabbed Chet's left hand just as he raised his right and countered with a twenty-eight hundred dollar bid, but Simpson responded almost immediately with a bid of three thousand.

"I may have made things worse for us a few minutes ago," she whispered into Chet's ear.

"I know," he said. "We couldn't hear you all the way up on this hill but we sure saw you. I'd say you handled everything just fine, although Orville Simpson might just disagree. Thirty-two hundred!" Chet shouted.

"I've got thirty-two hundred, do I hear thirty-three, do I hear thirty-three? The auctioneer shouted.

"Thirty-five!" was Simpson's response as he turned and looked directly at Chet and Callie.

Chet was about to make his last bid of thirty-six hundred when he heard a voice on the far side of the crowd.

"Four thousand," the man shouted.

Simpson stretched his neck to see who would have that type of money. He didn't recognize him. No one from this part of the country would come to an auction wearing a three-piece suit and a Hamburg hat.

Chet turned to Callie and kissed her on her forehead. "That's it," he said. "We're tapped out. But it will be okay. I promise."

Callie was speechless. This was all my fault, she thought.

Simpson was furious—he had promised his "little girl" that he would come home with the deed to the farm. "Five thousand," he shouted.

Chet was just as curious as Simpson as he heard the bid continue to rise. He could barely hear the other bidder's voice. The man was bunched up with several others on the far side of the crowd.

Chet walked to the barn with Callie at his side. "I gotta see who the hell has more money than Simpson around here," he said. He climbed the outside ladder that led to the hayloft. As he turned in the direction of the voice he saw a man with a cane and a handlebar mustache make his counter.

"Fifty-five hundred dollars," he said.

Simpson countered, "fifty-eight hundred."

"Six thousand dollars," came the response.

Chet squinted and a grin appeared on his face. He climbed down where Callie waited.

"It's going to be all right," he said. "Trust me."

"Going once, going twice, going three times to the man in the gray suit," the auctioneer said.

The family walked up to Chet and Callie, all very sullen looking.

"I'm sorry son," Pops said. We thought you had a good chance at it. Simpson had it in for you. And that other man, what in the hills brought him here?" Pops said.

Orville Simpson was angry. How dare some stranger outbid him? But maybe he could still make good on the deal. As he walked up to the new owner he was surprised to see a man of only about twenty-five years old.

"Hello there, son," he said. "I'd be willing to take this place off your hands for sixty-five hundred. I can have a draft for you by the end of the day. By the way, my name is Orville Simpson. I run the sawmill here."

"R. Bartholomew Wainright III of New York," the man replied as he placed both hands on the crook of his hand-carved cherry wood cane.

Simpson was surprised the man had refused to reach out and shake his hand. Maybe it was just because he needed both hands on the can to keep his balance.

"There's no need to offer any more money. I won't accept it," Wainright said. "My father is in the hotel and restaurant business in New York and we are in desperate need of prime beef. This farm should meet our needs."

"Well sir, I know this land," Simpson said. "You could still let me harvest all the timber for you. We both could make a good profit and you could double the amount of cattle to graze."

"That would be rather foolish," Wainright said. "I've seen forests stripped back East and it has ruined the land for future use. Besides, I plan to take on a partner here who has an excellent background in all sorts of livestock—Chet Harbison. Do you know him?"

Simpson's face turned flush. "Look here, Mr. Wainright, you're not from these parts. Harbison was a reckless kid when he left here to fight in Cuba. When he came back he was worse. He just ain't right in the head. He's threatened my daughter with a gun and he almost killed a man up in town last year with his bare hands. You can't trust a fellow like that. And that gal he's marrying, she comes from bad seed. Her old man was a known con-artist."

Wainright grabbed the handle of his cane with his right hand and smashed the tip of it against a boulder next to where he stood. Simpson jumped back. The cane splintered leaving a point on the end. Wainright lifted the cane and poked Simpson in the chest with it while working hard at keeping his balance on his one good leg.

"Trust? I was shot in the heel by a Spaniard soldier in Cuba," Wainright said. "Chet Harbison dragged me through the jungle for miles, even though he was suffering from a severe bayonet wound himself. It took hours, but he got me to safety. I believe I can 'trust' him more than anyone I know.

And by the way, a new friend of mine, a Mr. George Timmons, tells me you are notorious for overcharging for your services at your sawmill. My family is friends with the J. I. Case family in Racine, Wisconsin. They originally came from New York, you know. I can have a brand new steam engine with all the woodcutting accessories I need in just a matter of weeks. It's my understanding I could do quite well if my prices were only five percent less than yours. You know customer loyalty only goes so far. I trust you'll be leaving and you will be taking that wagon full of barbed wire at the edge of my boundaries with you. Good day!"

Callie, along with Harbison family members and friends were following Chet as he rushed down the hill to meet the man in the gray suit and Hamburg hat. Simpson brushed by the group without saying a word, until he saw Smith and ordered him to take the wagon back to the mill.

"What the hell are you doing way out here Three Eyes?" Chet said.

"Well, Missouri, that's a hell of a way to greet your new business associate, or should I say, 'Put her there, partner'," he said as he reached out his hand and almost lost his balance, again.

"As you like to say, I 'took a notion' to surprise you and come to your wedding. I got here yesterday and my new friend, George, invited me to stay at his cottage. He informed me of the recent 'going-ons' that you've omitted from your letters."

Pete and Cody looked confused, but for some reason George seemed at ease for once.

"Boys, this is Chet's friend, Ritchie, from the Army Volunteers. His real name is Richard Bartholomew Wainright III, but Chet always calls him Three Eyes because of those funny Roman numbers behind his name kinda' look like the letter I."

Pops walked up to Ritchie to shake his hand, and then handed him his cane. "Here, son, you'd better take this. Looks like you taught old man Simpson a lesson or two with that broken one of yours."

"Well thank you Mr. Harbison," he said. "This is very unusual. Is it made of mahogany?"

"Son, if you're gettin' into the cattle business, you'll learn it's the most important part of it. This is called a bull-dick cane. Consider it a gift. You're about the same height as me and I got more of them back home."

Now with the cane in hand, Ritchie walked up to Callie, lifted her hand and kissed it. "Your future husband told me you were beautiful in his letters, but I had no idea how strong you were until I saw you force that blonde harlot off of our land. By the way, Missouri, you owe me three thousand dollars, if we're to be true partners. After the wedding, you'll have to come to New York with me for a week or so to sign the papers. I can put you two up at one of my father's hotels if that's all right with you Callie?

"By the way, as you know, Chet is an excellent equestrian, but I dare say he has quite a bit to learn about polo. Some of my friends and I played against him and some other cowboys. They were very good at breaking the rules a bit to compensate for their lack of knowledge of the game.

"From what George tells me, Chet has never mentioned his heroism since he returned. He was like that in New York as well—told me to quit mentioning it. But I understand he's been put to the test a few times since he came home."

By now Pete could no longer hold back. "Chet tells me you're one hell of a guy yourself, Ritchie. But let me ask, do you all talk funny like that in New York?"

"That's an odd question," Ritchie said. "I asked Chet the same thing about 'ya'll' from Missouri."

"Come on, Three Eyes," Chet said. "I bet Ma can have supper for as many people as we can fit into the house. We'll get a bunch of hams out of the smoke house. We're goin' ta fill the dining room, the kitchen, and the front porch with as many friends as we can to celebrate our partnership. And do I have a horse to show you! If you think those polo ponies of yours are something. Wait 'til you see Red, and then some of the best Morgan horses in the country. And our mules will put those ones we used in Cuba to shame. You're gonna have to get outta that suit. I've got some jeans you can wear. And Callie and I have a lot to show you about cattle!"

For the next several days Chet and Callie gave Ritchie tours of the two farms. The two men discussed how it would be smart to start fattening up the steers with grain, along with pasture, for a month or two before herding them to the rail station and shipping them to a processing plant near the Wainright restaurants.

"Father wanted to name one of the new restaurants the Herford Room, but I insisted that with the information you had given me in your letters that Black Angus beef was a better choice for our customers," he said. "It will now be called the Aberdeen Angus House. If the venture becomes successful we may want to increase the herd size. Would it be feasible to have your father cut back on his horse production and raise cattle instead? We're seeing more and more horseless carriages in New York.

"That's not gonna happen here," Chet said. "This is horse country, but we could find more land. You know Ritchie, George doesn't have much money, but I think he's got access to a good spread. He'd be a great guy to manage it. He may seem a little slow, but there aren't many who know about livestock as much as he does. Have you maybe mentioned that to him?"

"To be honest I haven't seen much of him since the auction," Ritchie said. "He's been in a neighboring town helping a lady with her farm. George has been coming back every few days for clean clothes, but in all truth I've had the cottage to myself most of the time."

"Well, I guess the old gal really needs the help, and George has never been one to turn down money for a hard day's work," Chet said.

"Old? Missouri, I believe you are mistaken or your friend hasn't been communicating with you much. That 'old gal' isn't that old. George said she was just a few years older than he was."

ANNA ROSE

Several hours later Cody found himself sitting on a bar stool at Wheeler's nursing a cold Falstaff, complaining about the heat and asking if anyone had seen George, who had promised to meet him there more than an hour ago. The older Harbison boy was just about to leave when George opened the screen door to the store and walked in asking Wheeler for a sarsaparilla.

"Sorry I'm late but I had a heap of work to do up the road a piece," George said as he sat down next to his friend.

"So what's so important George?"

George reached into his shirt pocket and pulled out an envelope containing an invitation to Callie's and Chet's wedding at the new church.

"Miss Callie, she gave me this really pretty piece of paper asking me to come to their wedding," George said.

"Well of course she did," Cody said. "You're like family. You knew you were going to be invited."

"I know, but, uh, uh, would it be all right if I brought someone with me? I know you all are goin' to have food after the wedding and I didn't know if it would be okay for someone to be with me eatin' it."

"George, you know we'll have plenty of food," Cody said. "Heck just about everybody from around here is comin' and you know they'll bring even more food then what Ma and Beth are making. Who are you bringin', one of the farm hands from up in Luebbering?"

"No, there ain't no farm hands up thar that I know."

"George who are you bringin'?"

"Well, uh, uh, I was wantin' to bring Mizzez Anna Rose Henschell, the lady I've been a workin' for over there, if'en that's okay. She's really nice to me and we get along really good. Her husband—he's been dead for a piece—he never let her leave the farm much and I been talkin' about how you're my best friend and that Chet and Callie, and Beth of course, that they'd be good friends for her to have too."

"I thought she was an old widow woman," Cody said.

"Well, that's true," George said. "She's three and a half years older than me, but she's real nice. She ain't one to tease like that Lori Simpson girl. She's real gentle and says I'm the best man she ever, uh, uh, has ever met. Her husband, the one that done died a couple of years ago, she thought he was nice. He was a teamster drivin' those loggin' wagons through here all the time and she said he was really friendly at first. But once they got married and moved onto her daddy's farm he started taken most of the farm profits and spending them on whiskey, and maybe even women. She heard that he spent time down at the roadhouse in Cedar Hill, and he was doin' more than drinkin' in thar.

"When she asked him about where all their money had gone and if it were true that he'd been with other women, he got mean and started beatin' on her all the time. She's even got a scar on her forehead. She combs her hair down, but I saw it when we were out in the wind fixin' a broken down gate together.

"That drinkin' of his, it really got the best of him finally. The loggin' company told Anna Rose that he was so snookered he didn't tie those logs down tight and the whole load came tumbling down on him. Killed him dead it did. And the loggin' company didn't give her any money—said he had been takin' what they call advances on his pay and he owed them money and they wanted it back. Her and her pa— he's all laid up—had to sell a bunch of their cows and hogs to keep from losing the farm. And now they don't have much to work with. But, I'm makin' it right and with that twenty-five dollars that Chet gave back to me I think I can get some hogs goin' there and then sell some from a litter and get some cows too."

"Why didn't you tell me about all of this before? I thought we were best friends."

"Uh, uh, Cody, you know that you're my very, very best friend. I'm sorry we didn't talk before, but I was afraid. Ya know, no woman has ever uh, uh, been nice to me exceptin' for Lori Simpson, and she wasn't really bein' nice. So when me and Anna Rose got to bein' uh, nice to each other I just didn't know for sure if it was real. But it is. She even thinks I'm smart the way I sit down and think a spell when I get stuck on somethin'. Ain't that somethin'? She thinks I'm smart."

"George, I do believe you're getting smarter every time I see you."

Cody slapped his friend on the back, accidentally a little too hard and almost knocked him off of his stool. George returned the slap a little harder than usual and Cody purposely lost his balance and fell to the floor. "George, I think you're getting stronger too."

"Mr. Frost, will you please get my best friend another soda pop and I'll have another draft. George, I can't wait to see this little filly of yours. She must be something else. You better bring her to the wedding 'cause I want ta have a dance with her when the fiddle music starts after the ceremony. And another thing, if she's short on cash like you say, you'd better pick her out a pretty dress at Nelson's so she won't have an excuse not to come. Why I bet Chet, you, and me will have the prettiest gals there!

"I can't believe the wedding is only a couple a days away," Cody said. "We've got folks from all over coming. Heck Ritchie is all the way from New York. And Mr. Langer from the dairy in St. Louis is coming with his wife."

NEW SHOES?

"Tom, I don't understand why we're leaving so late to drive all the way to the Harbison farm, I thought you were going to get Friday off," Margie Langer said as her husband placed the satchels onto the back of his spring wagon.

"That was my plan," he said. "But my new supervisor—the owner's son-in-law—decided I needed to stay a bit longer. Funny how that boy don't care for me much," he said with a grin. "Might've been that mule that I assigned to his milk wagon when I used to be his boss. But don't worry. We'll make it in plenty of time for the wedding. We'll hit House Springs by dark and the Webers have already said we can stay with them. We'll leave early tomorrow morning from there and be in Grubville by noon. The wedding doesn't start until two, so that will give us plenty of time to clean ourselves up.

"Byron said his house is getting kinda full with Chet's bride-to-be staying there. Said Chet got ordered to stay with his friend Pete so the girls could get the wedding dress done without him being around. We'll be stayin' with a Mr. Nelson and his wife Saturday night. They own the general store and told Byron we were welcome guests.

228

"That younger Harbison boy and his gal sure have been through a lot. Byron and Helen too with them losing that colored girl who had been with them for so long."

Tom snapped the reins and his two black matched Morgan mules answered his request. The quick clip-clop of their feet was a familiar sound to Tom and Margie. He had always preferred mules for their stamina and had never owned a horse throughout his adult life.

As the sun rose Saturday morning Tom and Margie were already on their way. The spring wagon reached the outskirts of Cedar Hill before ten o'clock and Tom spied a skinny barefoot boy standing by the shoreline of the Big River.

"Mister, I'll be glad to lead those mules across fer ya for only twenty-five cents," he said. "This here river has a lot of jagged rocks. You wouldn't want them fine mules of yours to stumble, would ya?"

"Well son, they're pretty sure-footed but since I'm in my Sunday-go-to-meeting clothes I'll gladly pay you the two bits for your services."

Tom stood up and reached into his pants pocket to find the leather coin purse that he had carried with him for much of his adult life. As he popped the snaps open the young man pulled a derringer from the backside of his waistband. "I'm a thinkin' I'll need a little bit more of your money since thar's two mules," the boy said as he continued to point the derringer. While wide in girth, Langer was an agile man. Margie had already reached for the buggy whip, but Tom placed his hand over hers and slowly moved his head back and forth as he looked at her.

"Sounds fair enough," Langer said calmly. "Will four bits do?"

The boy was caught off guard with Langer's easy-going demeanor. "I'll just take it all, mister. Langer held the coin purse out almost within the boy's reach. When the youngster leaned forward to grab it, Langer grabbed his wrist. The teenager flinched from the strong grasp and dropped the derringer from his other hand into the sandy dirt below. It felt like his arm was locked into a bear trap. He pulled with all of his might and both he and Langer fell to the shoreline.

Margie grabbed the reins tight to hold the nervous mules from running off and grimaced. "Thomas M. Langer, I just pressed that suit of yours Friday afternoon!"

"Just a moment dear, I'm just a tad busy!"

By now the coin purse was lying on the ground with its contents of pennies, nickels, dimes and quarters sprawled out alongside it. Tom was standing erect gripping the back of the boy's britches with his right hand and holding the collar of his thread-bare shirt with his left.

"Boy, you floppin' around like a darn bluegill ain't making it any easier on you… or me!"

Just then the boy's shirt began to rip from his torso and Tom let go reaching for another section of the boy's waistband.

"Son, if you keep this up, you're gonna be naked as a jaybird out here and it's gonna be a bit embarrassing for you and my darling wife!"

The boy was near exhaustion after his attempt to escape. He finally collapsed onto the dirt and broke down crying.

"Don't take me to jail, mister. They got my two brothers thar already and they're gonna hang 'em for sure. My other brother is already dead. Their horses and mule came back to our cabin on their own a while back but someone with papers took 'em, sayin' they had money owed to 'em, and since I didn't have any they were takin' the animals. There ain't any food and nobody will hire me, even to clean out the spittoons at the log tavern."

Tom lifted the boy onto the back of the wagon and Margie handed the youth a blanket to wrap around his shoulders.

"No one's going to put you in jail for tryin' to steal fifty cents son," Tom said in the same tone he used when trying to calm a nervous mule. "What's your name, boy?"

"Lester, Lester Spragg," the boy said timidly.

"Look here, Lester, don't you try running off. I just might know a place where you can find work and even a place to stay, but we've got a wedding to get to and that job for you is a few days off. You ride along with us for a bit and we'll sort this out."

Margie looked at Tom and nodded her head. Then she reached into her cloth valise and removed a sandwich wrapped in newspaper. "Lester, why don't you try to eat this. We've got plenty to go around." The boy took the sandwich that contained thick slices of Braunschweiger and cheese on dark brown bread. He had a strange look on his face when he took his first bite but continued devouring it until it was gone. Then he picked up the breadcrumbs from his lap and ate them with his fingers.

"Would you like another?" Margie asked.

"Yes ma'am!"

"When did you eat last?" Tom asked.

"I had a little of somethin' yesterday, but it didn't fill me up much," the boy said with his mouth still full of food.

Tom snapped the reins and the two black mules crossed the river without incident. "We've still got plenty of time," he said as he looked at his pocket watch and then he placed it back in his coat pocket.

Two hours later the wagon carrying the unlikely trio reached the general store in Grubville. Tom stepped down from the wagon, ordered the boy to stay put and told Maggie he'd be back shortly.

Nelson was behind the counter when Langer walked inside.

"Hello sir. My name is Tom Langer and I suppose you're Mr. Nelson."

The store clerk reached out his hand to shake and smiled. "Just call me Nelson—everyone else does. Did you have a rough trip? You look a bit ruffled."

Tom grinned and pointed to the boy in the back of his wagon. "Had a run-in with that young fella a ways back by the river. Margie and I know about his brothers. We're discussing about taking him back to the city and getting him a job at the dairy where I can try to set him straight. We got room at home too, but he don't seem too sure about coming with us from the way he's talking. Sounds like he's scared to death now that nobody's ordering him around. Can he stick around here during the wedding? I certainly can't take him down to Byron's or the church after what his brothers did! Besides, the boy's starvin' to death. He's already eaten three sandwiches."

"You and your wife get your things and take them upstairs," Nelson said. "I'll talk to the young'un. He knows me some."

The boy remained sitting in the back of the wagon, afraid to move after Tom and Margie took their luggage and went inside. Nelson walked out to the porch while untying his white apron that was part of his daily outfit. He was the only man in town since Carl Cavanaugh died who wore a white shirt and Sunday trousers all week long.

Nelson looked over at the boy as he scratched his chin. "Lester, it looks like you've gotten yourself into trouble without the help of your big brothers this time. Couldn't you behave yourself just a little?"

"I couldn't help it Mr. Nelson," he said. "Everything at the shack is gone and nobody down there will give me work. I had to do it."

Nelson shook his head. "That man upstairs is a good man. I don't know him personally but I've heard a lot about him.

He said he can take you back to the city, give you a home to stay in and place to work. When he leaves Sunday morning for St. Louis, I think you should go with him. It's a lot better than getting' thrown in an orphanage or a county workhouse. You got nothin' to stay around here for. Your two brothers won't be comin' back no matter what happens at the trial. And they ain't been anything but mean to you ever since you were born."

"He won't beat me?"

"No he won't do nothing of the sort," Nelson said.

"How am I goin' fit in with city folks? I'm wearing rags. I don't even own a shirt anymore! He tore mine to threads down by the river this mornin'."

"If Mr. Langer is willing to give you a chance, so am I. I got a cot in back of the store and a pile of wood that needs splittin' in the yard. Let's go in and see my missus about gettin' you something to eat. We have to leave for a couple hours. When I get back that wood better be chopped. If it is, I'll pay you with some new britches, a shirt, socks, and a pair of shoes."

"New shoes?"

"Yep, new shoes from the Brown Shoe Company in St. Louis," Nelson said with a glint in his eye.

"I ain't never owned a new pair of shoes before! I used to get an old pair from my brother every time winter set in," Lester said. "Why is everybody tryin' to be nice to me?"

"Everyone deserves a fresh start," Nelson said. "You didn't have much of a choice bein' raised by them ornery brothers of yours and maybe they didn't either with the way your pa raised 'em after their ma died givin' birth to you. But you can't blame anything that happens to you any more on your brothers or anyone else. You're your own man now. That Mr. Langer and his wife will be good folks to learn from. Let's go in and find you some clothes and those new shoes. I got to be leavin' for that wedding pretty soon."

GETTIN' HITCHED

Chet Harbison fidgeted with his shirt collar outside of the new Grubville Baptist Church as his brother Cody and Ritchie Wainright attempted to calm down the horses hitched to the Studebaker buggy as Pete McKinney tied a string of tin cans to the back of it.

"Damn it Pete, if you keep rattling those cans you're gonna' spook the horses and they'll run all the way to Dittmer before they settle down," Cody said.

"Is my tie straight? Do I look alright to go inside?" Chet asked.

"You look as good as any hayseed is gonna' look in them thar city clothes," Pete said as he tied the last knot. "You look almost as good as old Three Eyes does with that fancy suit of his."

"Come on, Missouri, your brother and I better get you into the back of the church. The wedding's going to be starting and you better be up front when that gal of yours starts walking down the aisle. I think we can trust Pete to not let that team run off."

Chet and Cody joined the preacher up front just as the pipe organ began to play.

Helen, holding little Cody, was joined by Byron and Ritchie in the front row. A wreath with a white ribbon with the name "Lize" printed on it lay in the vacant spot on the pew. First Beth walked down the aisle and found herself on the opposite side of the preacher. When the Wedding March started all eyes were on the young red-headed girl with freckles and green eyes as Mr. Lee walked her down the aisle, and then kissed her on the cheek as they reached the altar.

"As the new pastor of this beautiful church, I have been alerted, or warned, by many to expect donations in the form of livestock and baked goods—and most important to keep it short and sweet. But please, give me a little leeway to say that I am humbled by the honor of conducting the first wedding service in this church to one of the most deserving couples I have ever met. Under the circumstances that they have faced, many would not have had their strength. Furthermore…"

At that moment the preacher noticed the raised eyebrows of Wheeler Frost in the second row as he folded his arms across his chest looking directly at the minister.

The pastor reached for his white collar with his left index finger in an attempt to breathe a little easier on the warm May afternoon. "But enough of that… Dearly beloved, we are gathered here today to witness the union of Chester Harbison and Kathleen Cavanaugh in holy matrimony, which is an honorable estate, that is not to be entered into unadvisedly or lightly, but reverently and soberly. Do you Chester Harbison take…"

Ten minutes later, Wheeler Frost looked approvingly at his watch, and the preacher, as Chet escorted his bride down the aisle to the outside of the church to be joined by nearly all of the townsfolk and visitors.

Cody and Beth followed as the wedding party stood in the shade of a large oak tree shaking hands with well wishers. Nelson constantly interrupted them, informing the couple and their friends to stand perfectly still as he held his Brownie box camera and pushed the shutter button. "Did you hear it? It sounds like 'ko-dac' when you push the button," he said with smile on his face.

The group of friends began to splinter off into sections after the cake was cut and cups of bright red punch were poured. Pete walked over to the table where Callie and Chet sat.

"Pete I just want you to know that the door of our little cabin, and our home once it is built, will always be open to you," Callie said. "I may not be as good a cook as Mother Helen and Lize, but I've learned a lot and I expect you over for dinner and supper," she said, giving a sideways glance at Chet, who winked to acknowledge her proper naming of the meals.

Pete reached into his jacket pocket and removed a flask and poured a finger or two into Chet's cup. Then he stood up very straight with his chest out. "Mrs. Harbison, I'd be happy to sit at your table every day of the week and eat your cookin', but that won't be happening for a while." Then he sat down on the bench next to them and settled in with his familiar slouch. "Callie, I've been hangin' around this town my whole twenty years, mainly to keep an eye on this no-good husband of yours," he said rolling his eyes up to the sky. "I can't even count the number of times I've gotten him out of fixes that he caused all by his lonesome. But with you here, I know my services are no longer required. I heard all those yarns he told about what happened down at the Harbisons' when those desperados had you two cornered and I don't believe a word of it!"

Chet and Callie began to smile.

"Chet's pretty good at gettin' himself out of a fix if thar's someone smart like me tellin' him what ta do, and I know damned, uh, darned well it musta been you callin' the shots or old Chet would've been six foot under today," Pete said. "Yep, I guess he don't need my expert advice with you crackin' the whip and given him orders.

"I got my bags packed and I'm headin' fer Nome, Alaska, to strike it rich. They claim you can find gold nuggets along the shore just glitterin' in the sunlight."

The couple looked shocked, but Chet knew while Pete was good at telling yarns about past brawls he and Chet had taken on, he was dead serious about searching for gold. He had mentioned it on and off since they were children. He reached out and shook Pete's hand. Callie stood up and kissed Pete on his forehead. "You make sure you write and that you take care of yourself. It's awfully cold up there."

Beth and Cody were feeding cake icing with their fingers to little Cody when George Timmons walked up to them while holding a woman's hand.

"Cody, I uh, uh, don't want to steal any thunder from Chet and Callie, ya know, but I'd like you to meet my sweetheart Anna Rose Henschell," he said, this time looking directly at

Cody and Beth. "I've asked her to marry me and she said, "Yes". Would you be my best man? And Beth, I've told Anna Rose so much about you that she wants you to be that matron of honor gal."

Anna Rose looked down to the ground, almost in the same manner that George did when he was nervous. "George, he talks about how nice the Harbisons and Mr. Frost has been to him all of these years and it's so nice to finally meet you. You need to come up to the farm and see all the things George has done to fix it up."

By now Ritchie had joined them and had congratulated George and Anna Rose on their announcement.

"George, Cody tells me that there's good pasture up at Miss Henschell's but there is little livestock."

"Well, it's got really good land and water running through it. The grass has been growin' real good since the rain started this spring. I figure it could handle thirty head of cows or so and still have room to grow corn for silage, but it'll take a while to fix all the fences and buy good cattle."

"Well, let's talk up at Wheeler's before I leave for New York with Chet and Callie. I'm still looking to expand my beef ventures even further but I need to have someone I can trust while I'm in New York. I can tell you're that man. Of course, Miss Henschell and her father would need to be in on the discussion as well."

"We trust anything George would agree to," Anna Rose said. "I trust him with my heart so I can trust him with our land."

"Come on everybody! It's time to toast the bride and groom before they go on their way," Pete shouted. "If we don't do it now we just might have to hold a chivaree outside that cabin of theirs tonight!"

Chet shook his head vigorously and then whispered into Callie's ear about the rowdy rural tradition of shouting and singing that wasn't going to happen no matter what. He promised their wedding night would be without guests at the little cabin he had rented. She stared into Pete's eyes with a mischievous frown on her face.

"Just kidding Callie, just kidding," Pete said.

The crowd began to circle around the newly married couple as Pete ordered and waited for them to quiet down.

Helen stood next to Byron as he lit his pipe, sucking in air to keep the tobacco burning. "This had better be good," he said as he looked at his wife.

"Hush now!" she responded, placing her elbow into his side.

The family and friends began to quiet down. Tom and Margie stood and tickled little Cody with George and Anna Rose stood next to them waiting to hear what Pete would say. Wheeler, along with Cowan and Marcella Lee, Nelson, Ritchie, and even Dr. Bockelman were waiting patiently for the toast.

Pete raised his cup as high as he could and looked at Chet and Callie. "Here's to all who wish this couple well, and…"

Just then almost everyone, especially Pete, turned to look what was making the racket behind him. There on the dirt road in front of the church came a horseless carriage. The engine sputtered and chugged as it slowed down attempting to make the steep grade in the road. Behind the wheel of the steering rudder was none other than Orville Simpson. He wore a floppy white cap, goggles and a white duster even though the weather seemed to be more like mid-summer. Next to him sat Lori Simpson in a white dress and white bonnet with a parasol in one hand while her other hand covered her mouth as she coughed from the fumes. Orville squeezed the bulb horn on the side of the carriage as he revved the engine in an attempt to climb the remainder of the hill.

"What is that and who is that girl all dressed up? Anna Rose asked as she held George's arm, somewhat in fright.

"That's nobody important," George said as he held his fiancé's hand. "Nobody important at all."

Cody patted him on the back.

Chet shook his head in disgust. "I can't believe the timing of all of this," he said. "Those contraptions will never last."

"Time will tell, son," was the quiet response from Mr. Langer.

Then Chet kissed Callie. "The important thing is that we have each other." Callie nodded in agreement and smiled. Chet turned and pointed to Pete. "Okay, old buddy. Finish your speech. I believe you were about to direct some of your comments to the two going down the road in that rattle trap!"

Pete smiled. "You betcha friend! …And all the rest can go to…" And then Pete saw the preacher staring him down.

"And all the rest can go to... well, you all know what I mean."

71639962R00138

Made in the USA
Lexington, KY
22 November 2017